# MAGICAL MELONS

# MAGICAL MELONS

More Stories About

Caddie Woodlawn

by

Carol Ryrie Brink

COLLIER BOOKS
*A Division of Macmillan Publishing Co., Inc.*
*New York*

COLLIER MACMILLAN PUBLISHERS
*London*

Macmillan Publishing Co., Inc.
866 Third Avenue, New York, N.Y. 10022

Collier Macmillan Canada, Ltd.

Library of Congress catalog card number: 44-9999

*Magical Melons* is also published in an illustrated
hardcover edition by Macmillan Publishing Co., Inc.

Printed in the United States of America

First Collier Books edition 1972

ISBN 0-02-041960-0

10   9   8   7   6   5

# Contents

# Author's Note

My grandmother, who was the original Caddie Woodlawn, died in January, 1940. In a few more weeks she would have been eighty-six years of age. On the day she died she had made doughnuts in the morning, and repaired a lock on one of the house doors which nobody else in the house knew how to mend. That was typical of her full and useful life.

But, now that Caddie is gone, why should there be another book of stories about her childhood? There are two answers to that question. One is the bundle of notes lying on my desk, in which are jotted many of Caddie's memories of people and events that did not find a place in the first book, *Caddie Wood-*

*lawn.* The other answer lies in the letters which I have received from boys and girls asking for more Caddie Woodlawn stories. Nearly ten years have gone by since the first Caddie Woodlawn book appeared, and the girls and boys who were Caddie's first readers have now grown far beyond her. But letters continue to come from new readers.

Perhaps for the sake of the very newest readers, who may not yet have read the first book and who are meeting Caddie here for the first time, it would be well to introduce the Woodlawn family once again.

In 1857 Caddie's father brought his family from Boston to western Wisconsin, where he was to install a sawmill for the Carson and Rand Company on the Eau Galle River. At the time they came, three white families and a tribe of Indians comprised the little settlement. But after the mill was established many other settlers came, and the Woodlawns soon moved a few miles away to a farm near Dunnville on the Red Cedar River, where these stories take place.

Father, with his rough red hair and beard and his kind good humor, understood the children and was greatly beloved by them. They were a little more in awe of dark-haired Mother, whose temper was sometimes hasty and who wanted them always to remember that they belonged to Boston as well as to wild Wisconsin.

Clara, the eldest girl, was dark-haired, calm, and quiet, like her mother.

Tom, Caddie, and Warren came next, and they were the redheaded and adventurous ones. Because Caddie had been delicate as a little girl, Father had let her live an outdoor life with the boys. Instead of learning to make samplers and cook, she had learned how to ride horseback and plow. She had grown as strong and rugged as her two brothers, and as full of bright ideas.

After Caddie came Hetty, also a redhead but not quite old enough to be included in the adventures of the three inseparables. Hetty was the self-appointed newsbearer of the family, the one who always flew across the fields to be the first to tell. Behind her trotted gentle little Minnie, her faithful shadow. Last of the seven children was baby Joe. The three youngest children had all been born in Wisconsin.

We should not forget Nero, either, who was the Woodlawns' dog and who shared most of the adventures of Caddie, Tom, and Warren.

This book is perhaps not so much a collection of stories about Caddie as about the whole family; for you will find that one story is about Warren, two are about Hetty, and some are even about their neighbors. Yet all these stories grew out of memories of her childhood which Caddie shared with me when I was a small girl and she was my grandmother.

Only one story in this book does not belong to Caddie. Once when I was at a Book Fair a gentleman came up to me and said, "My father was a circuit rider in Wisconsin. I wonder if he could have been the one your grandmother knew." Then he told me a story which he said I might use if ever I cared to. It was a true story of something which had happened to his father. It was a good story, and I have been happy in this book to let Mr. Tanner, the circuit rider, tell it in very nearly the same way that it was told to me.

These stories cover a period of three years, from the fall of 1863 to the fall of 1866. The first book of Caddie Woodlawn covered one year, 1864–65. In the story called "Magical Melons," Tom would be about twelve, Caddie ten, and Warren eight. As the stories go along, the children will be growing older.

CAROL RYRIE BRINK

# MAGICAL MELONS

# 1

# Magical Melons

The barn was dark and mysterious on a rainy autumn day. The horses munched and stomped in their stalls, glad of a period of rest from fall plowing and hauling. The cows switched their tails and blew softly through their nostrils.

Tom, Caddie, and Warren Woodlawn had perched on the side of the box stall watching Robert Ireton and Tom Hill, the hired men, at their milking, and they had all helped with the feeding and cleaning of the stalls. Now that the chores were done, the two hired men made a dash for the kitchen to pass the time of day with Katie Conroy, the cook.

"Mind ye get yourselves into no mischief now," were Robert's parting words.

"It's a pity he said that," said Warren, "because I feel bad today."

"Is it your stomach or your head?" asked Caddie anxiously. "Let's see your tongue."

"No, I mean I feel like acting bad," said Warren cheerfully.

"It's the weather," said Tom. "But there's no use being bad about it. Let's play 'I Spy.'"

"Where?" asked Warren.

"In the haymow!" said Caddie.

"I wish we could find buried treasure or fight Indians or something exciting," said Warren.

"We'd *better* look at his tongue, Tom," said Caddie.

"All right," agreed Tom.

In a moment Warren found himself pinned down and reluctantly displaying his tongue.

"*A-wa-wa-wa-wa!*" said Warren resentfully, trying to free himself.

"There's something wrong with his speech, too," said Caddie, with twinkling eyes. "Listen to what funny noises he makes when he tries to talk."

"His tongue isn't coated," said Tom. "He'll pull through if he's careful how he behaves."

Warren arose with wounded dignity and brushed himself off.

"If Hetty was here she'd run and tell Mother on you, and I'd just as lief do it myself if it wasn't raining so hard."

"Come on! We were just having fun," said Caddie. "Let's go to the haymow and play 'I Spy.'"

They climbed the ladder into the vast, sweet-smelling loft. Here the rain drummed loudly on the roof and seemed to shut them completely away from the world outside. Up in the rafters, pigeons rustled and cooed. The summer's hay, piled high, made an excellent place in which to hide.

They drew straws to see who should first be "It," and Warren drew the unlucky straw. He put his head on his arm and leaned against the side of the barn with his eyes tightly shut.

"Five, *ten;* fifteen, *twenty;*
  Twenty-five, *thirty;* thirty-five, *forty;*
  Forty-five, *fifty;* fifty-five, *sixty;*
  Sixty-five, *seventy;* seventy-five, *eighty;*
  Eighty-five, *ninety;* ninety-five,
    *One hundred!*
  All who aren't ready, holler '*I.*'"

There was silence in the haymow. Warren uncovered his eyes and looked around him.

"Here I come!" he warned.

Still silence—not a straw moved. Warren began to go cautiously around the loft, trying not to get too far from the goal for fear that either of the others would steal back to it before he saw them. There was a suspicious-looking hummock of hay, and suddenly he saw a tiny edge of denim skirt sticking out of it.

"I spy!" shouted Warren. "Come out, Caddie Woodlawn! I spy!"

"How did you know I was in there?" cried Caddie, bursting out of the hay like an erupting volcano.

"One, two, three for me!" called Tom, patting the side of the barn. He had slipped into goal while Warren's back was turned. "Caddie's it!"

Still protesting that she couldn't imagine how Warren had found her, Caddie hid her eyes.

"Five, *ten*; fifteen, *twenty*—" she counted.

Warren and Tom dashed away to hide themselves. Warren ran for the back of the loft. It was harder to get in free from there, but it was also harder for the one who was "It" to find you.

"Eighty-five, *ninety*; ninety-five—"

Warren dived into the hay and, pulling it

hastily over him, lay still. He tried to stop his quick, excited breathing. To himself it sounded as loud as the railroad engine he had seen once in St. Louis. Slipping his hand down under him to make his position more secure, he suddenly encountered something smooth and rounded and very cold. Before he could stop himself he had let out a bloodcurdling yell and popped up through the straw like a jack-in-the-box.

Tom burst out of another hidey-hole, and Caddie—crying "I spy! I spy!"—came galloping over the hay after them.

"What's the matter, Warren?" asked Tom.

"There's something in here," babbled Warren. "I felt it. It's cold and slick."

"Aw, foolishness," said Tom. "How could there be anything cold and slick in the hay?"

"Maybe it's a snake," said Caddie hopefully, "or that buried treasure Warren was wanting."

Warren was digging feverishly in the hay.

"It was over here. I felt it all right, but it didn't wiggle. It must have been the treasure."

They all began to dig now, tossing the hay in a loose mound behind them. Suddenly they reached the "treasure" and sat back on their heels, marveling.

"Melons!" cried Caddie. "Watermelons! However did they get here?"

"But Father sold the last of the melons in town a month ago!" objected Tom reasonably.

Yet there they were, more than a dozen beautiful green- and yellow-striped watermelons, carefully hidden under the hay. Tom tapped them with his thumb and forefinger, and they seemed to be sound and in excellent condition.

"But listen!" marveled Warren. "The few melons that were left in the field frosted and turned rotten several weeks ago."

"I know," said Caddie. "How do you suppose they came here?"

Tom's eyes grew dreamy as they did when he was telling stories or reading his Hans Andersen.

"You remember about the girl in the fairy tale whose cruel stepmother sent her out in a paper dress in the snow to gather strawberries?"

"Yes," said Caddie in an awed voice. "And she brushed back the snow, and there were strawberries!"

"Maybe it's like that," said Tom. "We brush back the hay, and there are watermelons!"

"Can we eat them?" shouted Warren.

"Why not?" said Tom.

"Maybe we'd ought to ask someone first," said Caddie doubtfully.

"I think we'd better keep it a secret," said Tom. "You go and tell about magic things like that and—*whoosh!*—they vanish."

It was easy to believe in magic in the dark loft with shadows in all the corners and rain drumming on the roof. Besides, it would have been very inconvenient going to the house in the rain and hunting up someone to ask about the melons.

"And they wouldn't believe us anyway," said Warren sensibly. "They'd say 'Melons in the haymow? How silly!' We might as well enjoy ourselves."

Tom took out his pocket knife and selected a melon.

"Can you eat a third of one?" he asked. It was only a rhetorical question.

"Of course!" said Warren, and Caddie said, "What do you think?"

The magical melon was the best one they had ever tasted, although it had been an unusually good melon year. Mr. Woodlawn had planted the seeds in new ground, which was plowed that spring for the first time, and the season had been just right to bring the melons to successful fruition. They would not have seemed magical if it had not been long past the season for them.

When they had finished eating, Warren asked an embarrassing question.

"What are we going to do with the rinds?"

"There was another story about a little girl with a wicked stepmother," said Caddie. "She had to go out hungry to herd her goats, but, when she got there, a little table would spread itself full of wonderful food for her. When she had eaten all she wanted, she would say, 'Little table, vanish!' and it would disappear."

Tom closed his eyes and spread his hands over the melon rinds.

"Little melon rinds, vanish!" he said.

But, when he opened his eyes, there were the melon rinds as big as life.

"The trouble is we don't have a wicked stepmother," said Warren.

"I know!" said Caddie. "The pigs!"

When the rain began to slacken, they made a dash for the pigpen and, standing under a dripping pine tree, carefully fed the melon rinds to the pigs. The pigs grunted their approval. They liked magical melons, too.

The children re-covered the treasure with a thick layer of hay, and it was over a week before they thought of the melons again. Then, cautiously looking about to see that they were not observed, they climbed once more to the loft.

"Do you suppose they'll still be there?" asked Tom, whose firm belief in magic was founded upon its vanishing qualities.

"I dunno," said Warren and Caddie solemnly.

But, when they dug, the melons were still there and, of course, it would have been a pity not to have another feast. It was a clear, frosty day outside, and it seemed likely that their little sisters might be out.

"Be careful Hetty doesn't see us going to the pigpen," said Tom. "She tells everything she sees."

"Why don't you want people to know, Tom?" asked Caddie.

"It would spoil all the fun to have the whole lot of them trailing up to the haymow after us. The melons would be sure to vanish then."

"Or if they didn't," said Warren sagely, "we'd have to cut each melon into more pieces."

So the two boys posted themselves as lookouts on either side of the pigpen, to give warning of anybody's approach, while Caddie

hastily thrust the rinds through the slats of
the pen and made sure that the pigs finished
them.

Almost every week now another melon followed its predecessors down the "little red
lanes" of Warren, Caddie, and Tom, and almost every week the treasure under the hay
grew smaller. For, strange as it may seem, the
good fairy who made watermelons grow in
haylofts did *not* continually replenish the
supply as one might expect a fairy to do.

One Sunday afternoon in late November,
Robert Ireton came to the living-room door
with his hat in his hand and a broad smile on
his pleasant Irish face.

"Begging your pardon, ma'am," he said to
Mrs. Woodlawn, "but me an' Tom Hill has a
little treat we've been savin' up for you and
the children. May we bring it in to you now?
And I'll be askin' ye just to have some plates
and forks ready for it when we come in,
ma'am."

The children were all atwitter in a moment.

"A treat, Robert? What kind of treat? Tell
us, please!"

But Robert and Tom Hill went out, smiling, without a word, leaving the children to
scurry about after the blue willowware plates

and the thin silver forks. For a mysterious Sunday-afternoon treat on a dull November day certainly deserved the best there was in the way of china and silverware.

"Father, do you know what it is?"

Mr. Woodlawn only shook his head.

Robert and Tom Hill were gone a long time, but finally they returned, looking much more sober than when they left, and each was carrying a beautiful big green-and-yellow-striped melon in his arms.

"Oh!" cried Caddie, a tragic note of disappointment in her voice. "They've found *our* melons!"

Robert put his melon on the table with a bang and looked at Caddie out of narrowed eyes.

"What do ye mean *we've* found *your* melons?" he demanded.

"Why, sure," said Warren, "those are our melons. We found them in the hay."

Tom said nothing at all.

"Well, how in the name of all the saints do ye think that they came in the hay then?" asked Robert, with flashing eyes. "Do ye think the fairies put them there, maybe, now?"

Here in the living room, with all the family looking on and the familiar blue and white plates on the familiar table, magic seemed to have deserted the three children completely, and Robert's sarcastic reference to the fairies suddenly put an end to the whole beautiful dream.

"So they was the culprits that meddled with our treat!" drawled Tom Hill. "Robert an' me was fair vexed that somebody had made off with more than half of the melons we had hid so careful."

Mr. and Mrs. Woodlawn, Clara, Hetty, and little Minnie had witnessed this scene with looks of the greatest puzzlement on their faces.

"Let's get this straight," said Mr. Woodlawn. "Melons in the hay? Fairies? Culprits? I'm afraid I don't understand."

"Well, sir," said Robert, "I don't know as you know it, but melons will keep a long time if they're packed in hay in a cool place. So, as there were more melons than could be used or sold, Hill here an' myself decided we'd bury a goodly number of them and bring them out as a surprise when the melon season was past."

"I begin to see light," said Mr. Woodlawn gravely. "And the treasure was discovered by pirates?"

"That's about the size of it, Misther Woodlawn," said Robert.

"How many of you children were in on this —this depredation?"

They knew what he meant, even if they had never heard such a big word for it. Solemnly Caddie, Tom, and Warren stepped out and hung their heads.

"We—we thought they were magical melons," blurted out Tom.

"Magical melons, indade!" said Robert.

"Well, I see only one just solution of this problem," said Mr. Woodlawn. "Whenever Robert and Tom are kind enough to bring us one of these melon treats, Tom, Caddie, and Warren will have to sit by and watch us enjoying ourselves without participating. Perhaps we can spare them any graver punishment. Does that seem proper, Robert?"

"Yes, sir," said Robert.

His kind face was already softening for the three culprits of whom he was so fond.

Sorrowfully Caddie set away three clean plates and three clean forks.

"I'm sorry, Robert," she said, "because I wouldn't like to rob a friend."

"There's just one thing," said Warren. "You'd ought to give the rinds to the chickens or the cows, because the pigs got all the good of the first ones."

"Pigs?" said Hetty, with a sniff. "Huh! I guess it was pigs all right!"

"And after this," said Tom piously as he watched the others sinking their forks into the beautiful red meat of the melons, "after this, I guess, we'd better ask before we eat."

# 2

# A Rare Provider

It was early in the winter of 1863 that Alex
McCormick got as far as Dunnville in western
Wisconsin with his flock of about a thousand
sheep. He had intended going farther west to
the open grazing land, but the roads of that
time were poor, and suddenly winter had
overtaken him before he reached his goal.
Snow had fallen in the morning, and now as
evening drew near, a low shaft of sunlight
broke through the clouds and made broad
golden bands across the snow. Where the
shadows fell, the snow looked as blue and
tranquil as a summer lake, but it was very
cold.

Caddie Woodlawn and her younger

brother, Warren, were perched on the rail fence in front of their father's farm, watching the sunset over the new snow while they waited for supper. Tom, who was two years older than Caddie, stood beside them with his elbows on the top rail, and beside him sat Nero, their dog.

> "Red sky at night,
> Sailor's delight,"

Tom said, wagging his head like a weather prophet.

"Yah," said Warren, "fair, but a lot colder tonight. I'd hate to have to spend the night out on the road."

"Listen!" said Caddie, holding up a finger. "There's a funny noise off over the hill. Do you hear something?"

"It sounds like bells," said Warren. "We didn't miss any of the cows tonight, did we?"

"No," said Tom. "Our bells don't sound like that. Besides, Nero wouldn't let a cow of ours get lost—even if *we* did."

Nero usually wagged his tail appreciatively when his name was mentioned, but now his ears were cocked forward as if he, too, were listening to something far away.

"It's sheep!" said Caddie after a moment's

pause. "Listen! They're all saying 'Baa—baa
—baa!' If it isn't sheep, I'll eat my best hat."

"The one with the feather?" asked Warren
incredulously.

"It *must* be sheep!" said Tom.

Pouring down the road like a slow gray
flood came the thousand sheep of Alex Mc-
Cormick. A couple of shaggy Scotch sheep
dogs ran about them, barking and keeping
them on the road. They were a sorry-looking
lot, tired and thin and crying from the long
days of walking, and their master, who rode
behind on a lame horse, was not much better.
He was a tall Scotsman, his lean face browned
like an Indian's and in startling contrast to
his faded blond hair and beard. His eyes were
as blue as the shadows on the snow, and they
burned strangely in the dark hollows of his
hungry-looking face.

"Will ye tell your Daddy I'd like to speak
wi' him?" he called as he came abreast of the
three children.

Tom dashed away, with a whoop, for Father, and soon the whole Woodlawn household had turned out to witness the curious
sight of nearly a thousand weary sheep mill-
ing about in the open space before the farm.
They had cows and horses and oxen, but none

of the pioneer farmers in the valley had yet brought in sheep.

Caddie and Warren stood upon the top rail, balancing themselves precariously and trying to count the sheep. Nero circled about, uncertain whether or not to be friendly with the strange dogs and deeply suspicious of the plaintive bleatings and baaings of the sheep.

Suddenly Caddie hopped off the fence in the midst of the sheep.

"Look, mister! There's something wrong with this one."

One of the ewes had dropped down in her tracks and looked as if she might be dying. But Mr. McCormick and Father were deep in conversation and paid no attention to her.

"Here, Caddie! Tom! Warren!" called Father. "We've got to help Mr. McCormick find shelter for his sheep tonight. Run to the neighbors and ask them if they can spare some barn or pasture room and come and help us."

The three children started off across the fields in different directions. As she raced across the light snow toward the Silbernagle farm, Caddie saw tracks ahead of her and, topping the first rise, she saw her little sister Hetty already on her way to tell Lida Silbernagle. Hetty's bonnet and her red knitted mittens flew behind her by their strings, for

Hetty never bothered with her bonnet or mittens when there was news to be spread. So Caddie veered north toward the Bunns'.

In a pioneer community everyone must work together for the common good and, although Alex McCormick was a stranger to them all, the men from the neighboring farms had soon gathered to help him save his weary sheep from the cold. With a great deal of shouting, barking, and bleating the flock was divided into small sections and driven off to different farms, where the sheep could shelter under haystacks or sheds through the cold night.

When the last sheep were being driven off, Caddie remembered the sick ewe and ran to see what had become of her. She still lay where she had fallen, her eyes half closed with weariness, her breath coming so feebly that it seemed as if she scarcely lived at all.

"Oh, look, Mr. McCormick!" called Caddie. "You ought to tend to this one or she'll be a goner."

"Hoots!" said the Scotsman. "I've no time to waste on a dead one with hundreds of live ones still on their legs and like to freeze to death the night."

"I've got lots of time, if you haven't, Mr. McCormick," volunteered Caddie.

"Verra good," said the Scotsman. "I'll give her to ye, lassie, if ye can save her life."

"Really?" cried Caddie, and then, "It's a bargain!"

In a moment she had enlisted the services of Tom and Warren, and they were staggering along under the dead weight of the helpless sheep. Their father watched them with a twinkle of amusement in his eye.

"And what are you going to do with that?" he asked.

"It's nothing but a sick sheep," said Tom "but Caddie thinks she can save it."

"Oh, Father," cried Caddie, "may I put her in the box stall and give her something to eat? She's just worn out and starved—that's all."

Father nodded and smiled.

"I'll look around at her later," he said.

But when Father had time later to visit the box stall, he found Caddie sitting with a lantern beside her ewe and looking very disconsolate.

"Father, I know she's hungry; but I can't make her eat. I don't know what to do."

Mr. Woodlawn knelt beside the animal and felt her all over for possible injuries. Then he opened her mouth and ran his finger gently over her gums.

"Well, Caddie," he said, "I guess you'll have to make her a set of false teeth."

"False teeth!" echoed Caddie. Then she stuck her own fingers in the ewe's mouth. "She hasn't any teeth!" she cried. "No wonder she couldn't chew hay! Whatever shall we do?"

Mr. Woodlawn looked thoughtfully into his small daughter's worried face.

"Well," he said, "it would be quite a task, and I don't know whether you want to undertake it."

"Yes, I do," said Caddie. "Tell me what."

"Mother has more of those small potatoes than she can use this winter. Get her to cook some of them for you until they are quite soft, and mix them with bran and milk into a mash. I think you can pull your old sheep through on that. But it will be an everyday job, like taking care of a baby. You'll find it pretty tiresome."

"Oh! But, Father, it's better than having her die!"

That evening Mr. McCormick stayed for supper with them. It was not often that they had a stranger from outside as their guest, and their eager faces turned toward him around the lamplit table. Father and Mother at each end of the table, with the six children ranged around; and Robert Ireton, the hired man, and Katie Conroy, the hired girl, there, too— they made an appreciative audience. Mr. McCormick's tongue, with its rich Scotch burr, was loosened to relate for them the story of his long journey from the East with his sheep. He told how Indians had stolen some and wolves others, how the herdsman he had brought with him had caught a fever and died on the way and was buried at the edge of an Indian village, how they had forded streams and weathered a tornado.

While the dishes were being cleared away, the Scotsman took Hetty and little Minnie on his knees and told them about the little thatched home in Scotland where he had been born. Then he opened a wallet, which he had inside his buckskin shirt, to show them some treasure which he kept there. They all crowded around to see, and it was only a bit of dried heather which had come from Scotland.

As the stranger talked, Caddie's mind kept going to the box stall in the barn; and something warm and pleasant sang inside her.

"She ate the potato mash," she thought. "If I take good care of her she'll live, and it will be all because of me! I love her more than any pet I've got—except, of course, Nero."

The next day the muddy, trampled place where the sheep had been was white with fresh snow, and Mr. McCormick set out for Dunnville to try to sell as many of his sheep as he could. Winter had overtaken him too soon, and after all his long journey he found himself still far from open grazing land and without sheds or shelter to keep the sheep over the winter. But Dunnville was a small place, and he could sell only a very small part of his huge flock. When he had disposed of all he could, he made an agreement with Mr. Woodlawn and the other farmers that they might keep as many of his sheep as they could feed and shelter over the winter, if they would give him half of the wool and half of the lambs in the spring.

"How about mine?" asked Caddie.

Mr. McCormick laughed.

"Nay, lassie," he said. "You've earned the old ewe fair an' square, and everything that belongs to her."

The old ewe was on her feet now, and baaing and nuzzling Caddie's hand whenever Caddie came near her. That was a busy winter for Caddie. Before school in the morning and after school in the evening, there were always mashes of vegetables and bran to be cooked up for Nanny.

"You'll get tired doing that," said Tom.

"Nanny!" scoffed Warren. "That's a name for a goat."

"No," said Caddie firmly. "That's a name for Caddie Woodlawn's sheep, and you see if I get tired of feeding her!"

When the days began to lengthen and grow warmer toward the end of February, Caddie turned Nanny out during the day with the other .sheep. At first she tied a red woolen string about Nanny's neck, for even if one loves them, sheep are very much alike, and Caddie did not want to lose her own. But really that was quite unnecessary, for as soon as Nanny saw her coming with a pan of mash and an iron spoon she broke away from the others and made a beeline for Caddie. At night she came to the barn and waited for Caddie to let her in.

One morning in March, when Caddie had risen early to serve Nanny's breakfast before she went to school, Robert came out of the barn to meet her. She had flung Mother's shawl on over her pinafore, and the pan of warm mash which she carried steamed cozily in the chill spring air.

For once Robert was neither singing nor whistling at his work, and he looked at Caddie with such a mixture of sorrow and glad tid-

ings on his honest Irish face that Caddie
stopped short.

"Something's happened!" she cried.

"Aye. Faith, an' you may well say so, Miss
Caddie," said Robert seriously.

Caddie's heart almost stopped beating for a
moment. Something had happened to Nanny!
In a daze of apprehension she ran into the
barn.

"You're not to feel too grieved now,
mavourneen," said Robert, coming after her.
"You did more for the poor beast than any
other body would have done."

But words meant nothing to Caddie now,
for in solemn truth the thin thread of life
which she had coaxed along in the sick sheep
all winter had finally ebbed away and Nanny
was dead. Caddie flung away the pan of mash
and knelt down beside the old sheep. She
could not speak or make a sound, but the hot
tears ran down her cheeks and tasted salty on
her lips. Her heart felt ready to burst with
sorrow.

"Wurra! Wurra! Wurra!" said Robert sym-
pathetically, leaning over the side of the stall
and looking down on them. "But 'tis an ill
wind blows nobody good. Why don't ye look
around an' see the good the ill wind has been
a-blowing of you?"

Caddie shook her head, squeezing her eyes tight shut to keep the tears from flowing so fast.

"Look!" he urged again.

Robert had come into the stall and thrust something soft and warm under her hand. The something soft and warm stirred, and a faint small voice said, *"Ma-a-a-a!"*

"Look!" said Robert. "Its Ma is dead, and faith, if 'tis not a-callin' *you* Ma! It knows which side its bread is buttered on."

Caddie opened her eyes in astonishment. Her tears had suddenly ceased to flow, for Robert had put into her arms something so young and helpless and so lovable that half of her sorrow was already swept away.

"It's a lamb!" said Caddie, half to herself, and then to Robert, "Is it—Nanny's?"

"Aye," said Robert, "it is that. But Nanny was too tired to mother it. 'Sure an' 'tis all right for me to go to sleep an' leave it,' says Nanny to herself, 'for Caddie Woodlawn is a rare provider.' "

Caddie wrapped the shawl around her baby and cradled the small shivering creature in her arms.

"Potato mash won't do," she was saying to herself. "Warm milk is what it needs, and maybe Mother will give me one of baby Joe's bottles to make the feeding easier."

The lamb cuddled warmly and closely against her. "Ma-a-a-a!" it said.

"Oh, yes, I will be!" Caddie whispered back.

# 3

## O Gentle Spring!

Spring is a wonderful season for ideas. In the spring Caddie's ideas surged up like the sap in the red twig dogwood and the scrub willow. The rising sap made the willow twigs golden yellow and the dogwood red; Caddie's ideas made her cheeks glow and her eyes sparkle. She saw the lambs leaping and dancing in the upper pasture, and it seemed that her numerous ideas sprang up also with joyous bounds and curvettings.

Her eyes took in everything in the changing landscape. She saw the arbutus at the edge of the snow, and the skunk cabbage with its solitary, clownish blossom. She saw last year's cattails standing fuzzy and frayed at the edge of the marsh near the schoolhouse. She saw that they had lost their bright, fresh brown color and that they were swollen with moisture and ready to release their seeds upon the wind. Caddie knew from experience that if you knock old cattails together their downy fuzz flies off like the fur of fighting cats. Something about this whimsical thought made Caddie pause and look again—and one of her bright ideas rose gay and sparkling to the surface of her mind.

That was the year when Miss Parker had first come to teach the Dunnville school for three months in winter and two months in summer. Miss Parker had not yet had her battle with Obediah Jones as to who should rule the schoolroom. Obediah and his brother Ashur were taller than Miss Parker; they were the biggest boys in school, and they never let anybody forget it. That winter the boys of school had taken sides. Some followed the two bullies; others followed Tom and George Custis in opposition to the Jones brothers.

Warren, of course, was on Tom's side, along with Sam Flusher and Silas Bunn. It did not take long for the girls' sympathies to be as sharply divided as the boys', and Caddie, Maggie Bunn and Jane Flusher formed a sort of ladies' auxiliary to Tom's forces—not that they had ever been invited to do so, of course. The boys wanted no hangers-on in petticoats, you may be sure, and any assistance the girls might offer was purely voluntary. For, although Tom, Caddie, and Warren were as thick as hops at home, at school with the other boys Tom had to maintain a decent show of scorn toward women.

Caddie couldn't help resenting this a little, because she felt, with some justice, that she was as accomplished in men's arts as any of them. Couldn't she plow, couldn't she whittle a willow whistle, couldn't she ride a wild horse bareback, as well as any of them? The answer, of course, was yes.

Yet all through the furious snow battles which had been waged that winter between Tom's and Obediah's forces, Caddie had had to stand on the side lines or content herself with manufacturing snowballs inside the fort. If she made tactical suggestions or began hurling snowballs herself, Tom said, "Say, you keep out of this. This is no fight for girls." George would have let Caddie in on an equal footing with the boys, but Tom said, "No. Ma will skin me alive if I let her get a black eye. She's got to stay out. This is men's work."

The worst of it was that Obediah's side was nearly always victorious. If it had been a contest in spelling or arithmetic, Tom's side would have had an easy victory; but outdoors on the schoolgrounds the Jones boys' superior size and toughness gave them the advantage.

It usually happened (accidentally, I suppose) that Miss Parker's bell rang just in time to save Tom's warriors from serious injury. But during the last snow battle of the season Ashur had tied up the clapper of Teacher's bell and, before she could get it untied again, Tom's crowd had suffered a black eye, a cut lip, and numerous bruises. Caddie felt shame for them. She also longed to see the Jones boys humbled. But before anything further was done the snow had all vanished like magic, and spring was at hand.

With the melting snow had come a truce and an interval of peace which must have raised poor Teacher's hopes.

School was almost over now for the season. Soon the boys would have to stay at home to help with the plowing and seeding, and the weeds could grow untrampled in the empty schoolhouse yard until the summer days when work was slack again and school would be resumed.

It was just at this moment in the spring that Caddie saw the innocent, sweet cattails standing thick and promising in the marsh behind the schoolhouse.

"Millions of them," Caddie said to Maggie, pointing them out.

"Millions of them!" breathed Maggie.

"They've been there all winter, too," said Jane, "and we never even saw them!"

During several recess periods thereafter the girls were busy cutting cattails and storing them under the schoolhouse steps. They carried them tenderly, like sleeping babes, so that none of the loosened fuzz should be disturbed.

One or two of the younger boys asked "Watcha doing?" and the girls were vague in their replies—something about stuffing for doll pillows, it seemed. The older boys were too scornful of feminine folly to pay the slightest attention to these preparations. They had their own concerns, for it seemed pretty certain that Obediah's crowd would not suffer school to close without a final showdown.

Still the last week passed uneventfully, and the closing program went down in history with nothing more remarkable to commemorate it than Caddie's spirited rendering of "Woodman, Spare That Tree."

But, when the last note of the last song had faded on the air, Obediah and Ashur were the first pupils out of the schoolhouse.

They went out grinning and whistling through their teeth, and Caddie said to Maggie and Jane, "*Now!* It better be *now*. We haven't got much time to lose."

They hurried into their coats and caps without bothering to gather up their books and slates. There was a scent of battle on the wind.

The first blow fell when Tom and George emerged from the schoolhouse with the rest of their crowd close at their heels. Obediah and Ashur were waiting outside. With nice timing each one thrust out a long-ill-clad foot just as Tom and George were reaching the last step. Tom and George had expected the attack to come from above rather than below. They were caught off their guard and promptly fell upon their noses in a very tidy but disconcerting manner.

Pushed from behind by some of Obediah's fellows, Warren, Silas, and Sam tripped over the prostrate bodies of Tom and George; and the whole of Tom's crowd suddenly found itself in a pile of flailing arms and legs, unable to arise and defend itself. Obediah's crowd now fell upon Tom's crowd with yelps of glee, and a tremendous uproar of shouting and howling arose which might have been heard as far as the Tavern on the other side of the river.

Caddie did not wait to tie her bonnet

strings. At the sound of battle she and Maggie and Jane burst out of the schoolhouse and began to pull their store of cattails out from under the school steps.

Thus armed, they darted into the edges of the fight and began beating Tom's opponents over the head with the fuzzy ends of the cattails. A long-stemmed cattail makes a surprisingly good weapon. Like a long thin rapier it allows the one who wields it to keep well out of range of his enemy's fists, and every blow is accompanied by a wonderful explosion of choking fuzz.

Obediah's warriors began to cough and choke and sneeze. Their eyes began to water. They were enveloped in a cloud of flying fur. Gradually they gave over trying to beat the life out of Tom's gang, and started to pursue the cattail wielders. Screams of the girls were added to the general hubbub. Now, in this instant's respite, Tom's men were on their feet again and hot after the girls' pursuers.

Cattail fighting is something which even the smallest scholars can take pleasure in. Hetty and the little Hankinson half-breeds and all of the younger boys and girls armed themselves with cattails and began to beat Obediah and Ashur and their sympathizers over the head with them. The air was hazy with flying fur, and a most enjoyable howling and yammering and sneezing arose to the blue spring heavens.

In vain Miss Parker clapped her hands and rang her bell. Her efforts only added to the general pandemonium.

At last Obediah and his fellows turned tail and ran, followed by a few persistent boys and by a trail of cattail fur. Some of the more enthusiastic members of the victorious party began beating one another over the head with cattails just for the pure delight of the sport, and because they hated to see a good thing come to an end. But fortunately the supply of cattails which the girls had cut was presently exhausted. The shouting began to subside, although the sneezing continued for some time. The children looked at one another and gradually their savagery gave place to laughter.

"Look at you!"

"Say, but you're a sight!"

"What'll your Ma say, anyhow!"

Miss Parker's neat and tidy scholars had turned into furry beasts. The cattail fuzz was stuck all over their woolen garments as securely as if it had grown there.

"All we need is tails," said Caddie.

Warren picked up a discarded cattail reed and began to wag it behind him like a tail.

"Look! Look! I've got one!" he shouted. "Look! I've got a tail!"

Victorious and pleased with themselves, the good children of school all caught up tails and began to wag them joyously behind them. In twos and threes and fours they took their various ways homeward, all of them prancing and capering, barking or yowling, and wagging their tails behind them.

So school dispersed that year, and the uncomprehending mothers of Dunnville welcomed home strange beasts whose sturdy homespun garments were coated for weeks with a mysterious fur which defied all brushing and shaking and hanging in the wind.

Wagging and prancing contentedly between Tom and George, Caddie suddenly remarked, "You know, Tom, cattails were my idea."

"It wasn't bad," said Tom. "I might have thought of it myself, only I didn't get around to it."

"I think it was pretty good," said George admiringly. "I think we'd ought to let her in on our side, Tom—honest I do."

"Well—" said Tom, his voice more friendly than his words, "I don't see how we're going to keep her out. It looks like she's in already."

Caddie gave her cattail tail an extra wag.

She had no idea what Mother would say at the appearance of her coat, but she knew that any punishment she might have to endure would be a small matter beside the satisfaction of seeing the fur fly around Obediah's ears and of hearing Tom say, "It looks like she's in already!"

# 4

# The Willow Basket

"They're shiftless—that's what they are!" said Mrs. Woodlawn decidedly.

Shiftless was a terrible word in pioneer Wisconsin. Caddie, Tom, and Warren exchanged discouraged glances. They had been delighted to see the McCantrys come back—even if the father, mother, and four children *had* returned on foot, wheeling all of their possessions in a wheelbarrow.

Mr. and Mrs. McCantry and the four children were standing in the road now, casting wistful glances at the Woodlawns' cozy white house while they waited for Tom and Caddie to inform their parents of their old neighbors' return.

"But, Mother," said Caddie, "Emma is so nice, and all they've got left is what they can carry in a wheelbarrow."

"They had just as good a chance here as the rest of us," said Mrs. Woodlawn severely. "They had a farm but they must needs sell it for what they could get and go on to something finer. And now, it seems, they are back with nothing but a wheelbarrow."

"We must not judge people too hastily, Harriet," said Mr. Woodlawn mildly, from the doorway.

"Oh, Father, we may ask them in for the night, mayn't we?" begged Caddie.

"Well, now," said Mr. Woodlawn, with a pleasant wink at Caddie over his wife's smooth dark head, "we'd better let the Mc-Cantrys go on to the next farm. The Bunns or the Silbernagles will take them in for the night, and that will let us out of any obligation."

Mrs. Woodlawn whirled about with a suspicious look in her eyes and was just in time to catch her husband's smile and the tail end of his wink.

"Go along with you!" she said, beginning to laugh. "I never intended to let them go without supper and a night's rest, and you know that. But I do feel better for having said what I think of them!"

Tom and Caddie and Warren raced away to invite the McCantrys in to supper and comfortable beds. They were a dispirited-looking lot as they sat along the roadside, waiting for the hospitality of a former neighbor. The bottom of Mrs. McCantry's dress was draggled with mud and dust, and the two boys were barefoot; but Mrs. McCantry had a bonnet of the latest fashion trimmed with purple velvet pansies, and Pearly, the little girl who was next to the youngest, had a new gold ring.

Emma, the eldest of the four and Caddie's own age, slipped a warm brown arm through Caddie's and gave her a squeeze. Emma didn't have gold rings or bonnets with pansies, but she was brown and solid and comfortable, and Caddie liked her best of them all. When a bird called out in the meadow, Emma could pucker up her lips and imitate it. It was Emma who looked after the little ones as much as her mother did.

Now Mr. McCantry picked up the handles of the wheelbarrow, and Caddie thought that his shoulders looked rounder and more bent than they had when he went away. The wheelbarrow creaked as he trundled it up the path to the front door. Caddie could see that it contained some patchwork quilts and cooking utensils, a set of Mrs. McCantry's hoops, and a clock which was not running.

"Why don't you wind your clock?" asked Caddie. "I hate to see a clock that doesn't go."

"It's broke," said Emma. "We still carry it around, but it's like most of the rest of our things. It won't work any more."

"That's too bad," said Caddie, but it gave her an idea.

Mr. and Mrs. Woodlawn met the McCantrys at the front door.

"Well, well," said Mr. Woodlawn heartily, shaking his former neighbor's hand, "so you have come back to us again, McCantry? Dunnville is a pretty good place after all."

"It is that!" said Mr. McCantry. "I'm glad to be back. We've been a weary way."

"Now, Josiah, why do you say that?" cried Mrs. McCantry sharply.

Caddie looked at her in surprise and saw that she had lost her discouraged look of a few moments ago and was quite the fine lady once again.

"We have had a most edifying journey really," she said, "and spent some months with my brother, who has a most elegant house which puts anything you have here in Dunnville quite to shame. Of course we were most elaborately entertained, and it is only by the merest chance that you see us in these cir-

cumstances. An unforeseen accident happened to our horse and carriage, and we just
thought how healthful it would be to come
along on foot."

"Yes, yes, of course," said Mrs. Woodlawn
hastily. "Now do come in and wash yourself
for supper."

The two little boys went along with Tom
and Warren—while Pearly was taken in
charge by Caddie's little sisters, Hetty and
Minnie.

Caddie squeezed Emma's arm.

"Come up to my room," she said.

"Wait," said Emma, smiling mysteriously.
"I've got a present for you, Caddie."

"A present for me?" Caddie was incredu-
lous.

"It's not very good," said Emma shyly, "but
I made it myself. An old lady who took us in
one night, when we hadn't any money,
showed me how."

She fumbled through the untidy bundle of
quilts and skillets in the wheelbarrow and
brought out a little willow basket.

"Why, it's ever so pretty!" cried Caddie,
sincerely pleased. "But you'd ought to keep it
for yourself."

"Oh, I can make lots more of them," said
Emma. "Big ones, too, but we don't have

room to carry them, and I thought you'd like this little one."

"I'd love it," said Caddie. "Thank you, Emma."

Meals were always good at the Woodlawns', but any sort of company rallied Mrs. Woodlawn to extra effort. Tonight, besides the supper which she had already planned, she went to the smokehouse and took down one of the hams which had come from their own well-fed pigs and had been salted and smoked under her own direction. With a sharp knife she cut the tender pink slices and fried them delicately brown before heaping them on the big blue china platter. Each slice was half ringed around with a delicate layer of fat— just enough to give variety to the lean. Mr. Woodlawn filled the plates of the hungry-looking McCantrys with the generosity of a good host, and Emma and the little boy fell to with a will. But Pearly set up a thin wail of protest.

"I can't eat this," she said, pointing an accusing finger at the fat.

"Me neither," said Ezra, the littlest brother.

"You can't eat that tender bit of fat?" cried Mrs. Woodlawn in surprise.

"They've got aristocratic stomachs," Mrs. McCantry said proudly.

For a moment Mrs. Woodlawn was speechless.

"Maybe Mama could cut the fat part off for
you, Pearly," began Mrs. McCantry doubtfully.

Mrs. Woodlawn's earrings began to tremble
as they always did when she was excited.

"No," she said, with that gleam in her eye
which her own children had learned to obey.
"If you can't eat that good ham just as it is, fat
and lean, you're not very hungry. My children eat what is set before them with a relish.
They know if they don't they can go to bed
empty. Anyone who eats at my table can do
the same."

Over her tumbler of milk Caddie saw with
twinkling eyes that Pearly and Ezra were eating their fat with their lean. Personally she
thought the fat was the best part when it was
all crisp on the outside and juicy on the inside, as Mother fried it.

The McCantrys were not there for one
night only; they stayed on for many days, but
there were no more complaints about their
meals.

Caddie and Emma enjoyed the time very
much. Together they went down to the
swamp where the young willows grew thickly,
and the boys helped them cut slender, pliant
shoots to weave more baskets. The Woodlawn

land and Dr. Nightingale's land came together here at the edge of the swamp, and beyond their fences the swamp stretched away in a fairyland of tiny hummocks and islands on which grew miniature firs and tamaracks. There were wild rice in the swamp in the autumn and quantities of wild cranberries.

"What a pretty place this is!" said Emma. "If I were you, Caddie, I would build a little house on this hill overlooking the swamp. I like the nice spicy swamp smell, don't you?"

A red-winged blackbird, swaying on a reed, uttered a throaty call, and Emma answered it.

Caddie remembered this later, when she heard her father and mother talking about a home for the McCantrys.

"Really, Harriet," said Mr. Woodlawn, "I've talked alone with McCantry, and they have reached rock bottom. He hasn't any money left."

"To hear *her* talk, you would think they were millionaires."

"I know, my dear, but she's a foolish woman. It's her foolishness that's brought them where they are, I think. But we can't let them starve for all that, and we can't have them living with us always either. Somehow we've got to set them on their feet once more."

"Well, Johnny, grumble as I may, I suppose that you are always right about such things. What had we better do?" sighed Mrs. Woodlawn.

"I thought we might give them a little land at the edge of our place somewhere. Perhaps one of our neighbors on the other side would contribute a little, too, and then all of the neighbors could get together and help build them a house. We could make a sort of raising bee out of it."

"A raising bee!" repeated Mrs. Woodlawn, her eyes beginning to shine. "Yes, we could do that."

"Oh, Father," cried Caddie, forgetting that she had not been included in the conversation so far, "that would be lots of fun! And I'll tell you the very place for the house."

"You will?" laughed her father. "So you've already picked the site?"

"Yes, I have! It's that corner down by the swamp. Emma loves the smell and the red-wing blackbirds, and they could get all the cranberries and wild rice they needed and maybe they could sell what they didn't need, and they could make willow baskets out of the willow shoots and sell those too."

"Willow baskets?" asked her father. "Sell willow baskets? You're going a little too fast for me, daughter. I'm lost in the swamp."

"Oh, wait!" cried Caddie. She was in one of her eager moods when ideas came too fast to be expressed. She flew out of the room and returned in a moment with Emma's basket in her hands. "Look! Wouldn't you pay money for a big basket, if it were as nicely made as that?"

Her mother took the basket in her own slender hands and looked it over carefully."

"Yes, I would," she said. "I believe a lot of people would. We've never had anyone around here who could make baskets."

"Well, we have now," said Caddie. "Can't we set the McCantrys up in business?"

"Where's my bonnet?" cried Mrs. Woodlawn. "I'm going to call on the neighbors!"

Dancing with excitement, Caddie ran for her mother's tasteful gray bonnet.

"Thank Kind Providence, it doesn't have purple pansies on it," said Mrs. Woodlawn as she went to the barn for a horse.

There was nothing like another's need to rally the pioneers of that day. Dr. Nightingale joined Mr. Woodlawn in donating a good-sized strip of land at the edge of the swamp. Another man, who had plenty of timber on his farm, offered enough logs to build a cabin if others would cut and haul them. Men and boys who had nothing to give but their time gladly did the cutting and hauling. One neighbor offered a pig, another a cow, and a third the use of his horse and plow to break a garden spot.

On the day of the "raising," men and boys on horseback arrived early from all the country around and went to work on the cabin. The women and girls came along later in the morning with covered dishes and jars of pickles and preserves.

Mrs. Woodlawn and Mrs. McCantry, with the help of the children, had made tables by putting long planks on sawhorses near the site of the new house. Over an open fire were great pots of coffee and stone jars full of Mrs. Woodlawn's choice baked beans.

It was not often that the neighbors came together for a common purpose. They were a settled community now, and it had been a long time since one of them had had a raising for himself. There had been the time of the Indian "Massacree Scare" when they had all come together under the Woodlawns' roof for several days, but then they had been filled with fear and distrust. Now they came together in a spirit of friendship and helpfulness.

The children raced about playing tag and

"Blindman's Buff" and "I Spy," while the men laid up stones for a fireplace and hewed and raised the logs one upon another to make the McCantrys' walls. The women unpacked baskets and laughed and chattered as they spread the feast. They were seeing friends and neighbors they had not seen for weeks, perhaps for months or years.

There was one thing which Mrs. Woodlawn and Mrs. McCantry had in common: they both loved a party. With happy, flushed faces they moved about among the neighbors, shaking hands, filling coffee cups, and urging more beans or gingerbread on people who had already eaten their fill.

The swamp echoed with the ringing of axes and mallets and the cries of men as they heaved the upper logs into place. By sundown the McCantrys had a house of their own. All the hard work was done and only the finishing was left for Mr. McCantry. As the neighbors prepared to depart, other gifts came out of their wagons: a sack of potatoes, a rocking chair, a bushel of turnips, a goosefeather pillow, strings of dried apples, a couple of live chickens.

At the last moment Mr. Woodlawn nailed up a shelf by the new fireplace. No one knew why until Caddie and Emma came breath-

lessly over the fields from the Woodlawns'
house carrying the McCantrys' clock. Caddie
and her father had sat up late in the attic shop
the night before to take it all apart, clean it,
and coax it to run. Now it ticked away on the
shelf as gay as a cricket.

"There!" said Caddie triumphantly. "A
house is ready to live in when a clock is tick-
ing in it!"

"My land!" said Mrs. McCantry. "That
clock hasn't ticked for years—just like us, I
guess." Her bonnet was all crooked with excitement and the purple pansies bobbed and
trembled over one ear, but for once her eyes
were perfectly frank and honest. "I know
what you've been thinking of us, Mrs. Woodlawn," she said slowly. "Shiftless, you
thought, and I guess you were right. But
we've seen what neighbors can be like today.
We're going to set right out to be good neighbors ourselves. You won't ever regret all that
you have done for us!"

The two women looked at each other and
for the first time they smiled in sudden understanding. Caddie and Emma smiled at
each other, too, and hugged each other.

Caddie knew that Mrs. McCantry might
often forget her good resolutions, for she was
that kind of person; but she knew also that

Emma would always make up for Mrs. Mc-Cantry's shortcomings, for Emma was a person to trust.

The McCantrys would be good neighbors.

# 5

## Animal Kingdom

Everybody likes a pet to care for and love. Of
course Nero belonged to the whole family,
and there were always young pigs and calves
and colts on the farm, but still a personal pet
was always welcome in the Woodlawn family.

Caddie had had her old sheep, Nanny, and
now she had her very own lamb, which she
had christened Bouncer.

Hetty and Minnie had a pet chicken, which
drew a little cart for them by means of a
string harness. In the fall, when Father had
banked the foundation of the house for winter, one of the half-grown chickens had been
accidentally banked in under the house.

There were so many young chickens about that nobody missed this unfortunate one.

"There's a chicken cheeping and calling somewhere outside, as if it is in trouble," Mother had said several days later.

Everybody listened and, sure enough, they heard it. They hunted the place over for several more days with no success. The cheeping and crying always sounded farther away when they went out of doors. It was only in the kitchen that the sound came clear and loud. They searched on the kitchen roof, they tapped the kitchen walls, but it was only when they saw Nero cocking his ears and looking down at the kitchen floor that it occurred to anyone to remember the space between the floor and the ground.

Hetty was all for having up the kitchen floor at once to rescue the poor fowl, but Tom said, "No, it must have got through that open place in the foundation and been too frightened to come out while Father and Robert were banking the foundation with sod and straw. The thing to do is to pull away the banking from the open place, and someone crawl in there and get the chicken."

"Well, do as you like," said the cook, Mrs. Conroy, "so long as ye do it outside. But divil a bit will I let ye tear up my fine kitchen floor for the likes of a chicken."

By the time they had come to the decision to act on Tom's advice, the cries of the chicken had grown quite faint and faraway.

"Oh, hurry, Tom! Do!" Hetty cried. "The poor thing's dying of starvation!"

"Oh, dear!" said little Minnie. "The poor, poor thing!"

Tom and Warren and Caddie went out and dug away the banking from the open place in the foundation while Hetty and Minnie stood by and watched. But when the gap in the foundation rocks was laid bare, they all saw that it was a smaller hole than they had remembered. None of the three larger children could possibly have crawled in there; and certainly none of them wanted to, for the hole looked singularly dark and uninviting.

"Let's try putting some feed here, and calling *Chick! Chick!*" suggested Tom.

But—whether from fright or weakness they could not tell—the poor lost chicken would not be lured into the open air. Vainly they coaxed and peered into the darkness, but only an occasional weak chirp told them that the chicken was still there. They could see nothing.

"Maybe Hetty could get into the hole," Caddie suggested, and Hetty tried.

But she stuck fast and had to be pulled out

with muddy pantalets and many cries of anguish.

"I wonder about little Minnie," Tom said doubtfully.

Caddie shook her head, and Hetty cried, "It's dreadful in there! Minnie would be afraid."

They all looked at little Minnie and she looked back at them with her round blue eyes, and then suddenly she surprised everyone by saying in her small, shy voice, "I can."

Little Minnie was a tight fit, but they managed to get her through the hole into the darkness.

"Now don't you be afraid, Minnie," Hetty called anxiously. "There's nothing in there to hurt you, honey. Don't you be a bit afraid."

Little Minnie turned around and put her face out of the hole for a moment to console Hetty.

"It's all right, Hetty," she said seriously. "Don't you be afraid either, honey."

Little Minnie was gone for so long a time that even Tom began to be worried.

"Golly! What would Ma say if we lost her?"

"Well, maybe Katie Conroy would let us take up the kitchen floor for *Minnie*," Caddie said.

"Minnie! Are you all right?"

"Yes," replied little Minnie's voice from far under the house, and presently, all covered with cobwebs and dirt, she came crawling out with a half-dead chicken in her arms.

That was how Hetty and Minnie got their special pet.

For a long time the chicken took not the slightest interest in life, but squatted dejectedly in the cotton-lined box which the little girls provided for a bed and pecked halfheartedly at their offerings of food and water. When he finally made up his mind that life was worth living after all, the snow had come and nobody had the heart to turn him out into the cold. Tom made him a little pen behind the woodbox; and when he was not in it he was riding around on Hetty's or Minnie's shoulder, or pulling their penny dolls in a little cardboard cart which Caddie constructed from a discarded box.

"The girls have got all these pets," Warren said. "Tom, we'd ought to have something, too."

"I know," Tom said. "But what?"

"Tadpoles," Warren suggested, and added more thoughtfully, "snakes, maybe."

But there is a singular lack of warmth and response in the affection of a tadpole or a snake.

In February, when they went through the

woods tapping the hard maple trees and hanging their buckets on pegs to catch the maple sap, they often saw the speckled sides or short white tails of the deer vanishing away through the hazel brush.

"A deer, now—" Tom said. *"That* would be a pet if you could get one! Tadpoles and snakes—they wouldn't be in it!"

But the boys were still looking for the ideal pet when spring came and with it the shearing of the sheep.

Caddie's Bouncer was a year old that spring and had as fine a coat of wool as any animal in Father's flock, which now numbered nearly seven hundred and fifty sheep. Caddie was looking forward to the money she would get from Bouncer's wool after the shearing, for, as well as being a delightful pet, Bouncer was also Caddie's fortune.

Before the shearing started, Father came home with the news that wool was worth sixteen cents more a pound if it was washed before it was sheared.

"We're going to wash all of our sheep," Father said.

"Seven hundred and fifty sheep?" cried Mother. "My dear, you must have lost your wits!"

"Not at all," said Father. "I've thought it

all out. We'll build large pens near the sand bar on the river and, as soon as the weather is warm enough, we'll begin washing the sheep there. We'll turn them into the clean green pasture to dry before the shearing. I can get a couple of extra men from town to help the hired men and myself, and of course the boys can help."

"And me, Father!" Caddie cried. "Surely you'll let me do it, too!"

"Well," said Father, "we'll see how you do with Bouncer. If you can handle him, I guess that you can handle anything."

"Of course, I can handle Bouncer!" Caddie cried. "My very own lamb!"

If words sounded very certain, she may have felt somewhat less certain within herself. For Bouncer was big and strong this spring and not so easily handled as when he had lain in her arms, a helpless, motherless baby.

The barrel of soft soap, which Mother and Katie Conroy had made from waste fats and wood ashes, was trundled down to the new pens near the sand bar on the first warm day of spring, and the washing of the sheep was begun. For a while Caddie stood and watched Tom and Warren hanging on to a sheep by a strap round its neck while they poured water and a handful of soft soap over its back and

worked up a lather. The more difficult part of
the procedure came when they had to entice
the creature into the river for a thorough
rinse before driving it up again onto the sand
bar and along a little runway to the pasture.
The men and boys had worn their oldest
clothes, and it was not long before they were
as wet as the washed sheep.

The sheep were nervous and alarmed by
these unusual proceedings. They jumped and
plunged and tried to run away in the wrong
direction. It did not help matters a bit that
someone was hunting on the opposite bank of
the river. The occasional sound of a shot in
the distance only frightened the timid sheep
the more.

"Autumn's the time for hunting," Robert
Ireton grumbled. "Bedad, this is no time to
be out flinging shots about! The lad had better be washing sheep."

But whoever was at work in the woods opposite seemed to have his own opinion in the
matter, for the shooting continued for some
time.

Father looked at Caddie as he finished a
particularly lively sheep.

"You'd better change your mind, daughter," Father called. "I'll wash Bouncer for you
myself."

Caddie only shook her head and was ready for Bouncer when he came out of the pen. A long time ago she had painted a bright red spot on his forehead, so that nobody should ever mistake him for anyone else's lamb.

She flung the strap about his neck as she had seen the boys do and, talking softly to him, got him to the edge of the water. But here he gave a sudden leap and change of direction, and it was all she could do to hold him down by flinging herself across his back and sinking frantic fingers into his wool. After a moment he stood still again, and she was able to pour the water over him. Warren helped her with the soap, and as she worked it into his wool she could see how fine and white it was going to be when it was rinsed.

"Sixteen cents more a pound, Bouncer," Caddie said, "and—my!—won't you look funny when it's all cut off? Come on now, baby, into the river with you! You're going to be a beauty when I'm through with you."

Bouncer had other ideas about the river. He tried to run in every direction but the right one. Tom and Warren, shouting and waving him back toward the water, drove him even more frantic. In the excitement Caddie lost the strap from his neck and could keep hold of him only by sinking her fingers deep

in his wool. She did not let him get away, but
although the two of them were firmly at-
tached, it became more and more apparent
that Bouncer and not Caddie was in control.

Seeing that all other avenues of escape were
closed, Bouncer finally took to the river with
Caddie still hanging on for dear life. But he
did not come docilely to land, on the sand
bar, and into the pen as the other sheep were
doing. He suddenly struck out into mid-
stream, swimming strongly, and Caddie—alas!
—went with him.

Above the sound of rushing water she
heard Father's voice crying out, "Hold on to
him! Hold on to him! I'm coming."

My goodness! She couldn't have let go of
him now if she had tried. Away they went,
headed directly for the opposite bank of the
river.

The canoe was drawn up near the sand bar
in case of emergency, and in a moment Father
and the boys were in it and paddling up into
the current as fast as they could after Caddie
and Bouncer. But Bouncer reached shore before they did and, when they came up, they
saw that Caddie had flung herself on top of
her sheep and was desperately preventing him
from running off into the woods.

Dripping with water and red in the face

from her exertions, she nevertheless shouted triumphantly at Father, "I handled him, Father! I handled him. I guess I can handle anything!"

When Father had secured Bouncer firmly with his own strap, he began to laugh.

"Yes, you handled him," he said. "But if you don't get to the house now, and into some dry clothes, I can tell you that your mother will handle *me* and not too gently either."

"Oh, Father, Father!" wailed Caddie. "You aren't going to make me stop washing sheep?"

"Well, child, you come back in half an hour in dry clothes, and maybe I'll give you some gentle old ewes to wash," Father said, still laughing mightily.

He put Caddie into the canoe to paddle, and got in after her with a subdued sheep held firmly in his arms. The boys shoved them off.

"I'll send Robert back after you in a few minutes, lads," Father called to them as the canoe took off for the scene of the sheep washing.

"Don't hurry," Tom replied. "We'll go see who was shooting."

"The shooting's stopped now, Tom," said Warren. "I haven't heard one for a long time."

Nevertheless they struck into the woods beyond the riverbank, with their eyes and ears alert for signs of the hunters.

"I think, like Robert," said Tom, "this is a bad time of year to hunt. It's the time of year for mothers and young things that didn't ought to be killed."

"One of those back-East fellows, maybe," said Warren, "who don't know how to carry on with a gun in the West."

They went on for a short distance in silence until they came to a small mossy opening under the trees. There were Mayflowers and bloodroot in blossom among the mosses and last year's leaves; and fronds of fern, like little rearing heads, were beginning to uncurl. In the midst of all this gentleness and beauty lay the carcass of a newly killed deer.

"He's stripped off the haunches for meat and left the rest of the carcass to waste," said Tom angrily.

"I guess he took the antlers, too," said Warren. "I don't see 'em."

Tom went around to the animal's head.

"No," he said. "It never had any antlers; it's a doe. Warren, I bet she had a fawn! At this time of year every doe has got a little one. Oh, golly, what a rotten thing to do!"

Softly they went through the underbrush

looking for the fawn. Its white spots on brown were like the small white flowers on the brown leaves. Tom looked at it for almost a minute before he really saw it. It was lying very quiet there where its mother had left it, and keeping very still as she had taught it to keep.

Tom knelt beside it and his hands were slow and gentle in their movements so that he would not frighten it. He could hear Warren crashing through the brush near by.

He said in a quiet, warning voice, *"Warren!"*

"What? Did you find it, Tom? Did you find the fawn?"

"Quiet," Tom said.

"Oh, Tom!" whispered Warren, coming to stand beside him and look at the perfect little creature which lay trembling on its bed of leaves and flowers and ferns.

"The mother's dead," said Tom in a low voice. "I guess it hasn't anybody but us. Like Caddie's lamb."

"Can we raise it on a bottle, Tom, do you think?"

"Ya. George Custis raised one."

"What if the hunters get it, like they got its Ma?" whispered Warren fiercely, wiping his eyes and nose upon his sleeve.

"We'll put a red flannel band around its middle," Tom said, "so they'll know not to shoot."

Gently he lifted it and wrapped his coat around it.

"I guess we got our pet now, Tom," Warren said. "You guess so?"

"Ya, I guess so," said Tom.

They walked very softly through the woods carrying the fawn by turns, and their eyes shone with a new brightness.

# 6

## Emma Went Too

Caddie, Lida Silbernagle, and Emma Mc-
Cantry all started early to walk into Eau Galle
to see the Medicine Show. They were going to
have supper at Lida's Grandma's, and Mr.
Woodlawn was going to drive them home
after the show was over. Caddie's brothers had
gone to Eau Galle with Father in the morning.

Caddie had on her good blue dress and
Lida a new bonnet with artificial cherries on
it. Emma didn't have anything new to wear,
but she felt lucky enough to be getting to go
at all. There were always so many things to do
at home which Mrs. McCantry didn't like to
do because they spoiled her hands. But nei-

ther Emma nor Mrs. McCantry cared how
Emma's hands looked, so it was often hard to
get away. Of course Emma had the eggs to
deliver to the crossroads store on the way, and
the candle mold to return to Grandma Butler
at the second farm before the crossroads, and
the Star of Bethlehem quilt pattern to borrow
from the blacksmith's wife; but she did *not*
have to take a baby along to mind and that
was something. Emma sighed. It wasn't that
she minded looking after the younger children or running her mother's errands, but it
was so nice to have a day to herself once in a
while, and time to go somewhere with the
other girls.

"They say it's a dandy show," said Caddie.
"Robert Ireton saw it in Durand last week.
The man who runs it is called Dr. Hearty,
and he sings and plays the banjo and does
sleight-of-hand tricks. He has an old spotted
horse and he carries his show along with him
in his wagon."

"Does he have a trick dog, too?" asked
Lida.

"Oh, yes. That's about the best part. They
say his medicine cures everything that you
could have, but I guess Dr. Nightingale
doesn't think much of it. Most people go to
see the show, not to buy the medicine."

"I'm sure I don't want any medicine," said Lida, "but it will be fun to hear banjo singing and see magic. Did a medicine show ever come out here before?"

"Not that I ever heard of."

Emma jogged along beside them with the basket of eggs on one arm and the candle mold under the other, and she didn't say a word but she kept smiling. She thought to herself that she had never seen a show at all and this was going to be quite wonderful. When they cut across the pasture a bobolink whistled at them, and Emma whistled back at it—a true bobolink call.

"I wish I could do that," said Caddie, puckering up her lips to try.

"Emma can make lots of birds' whistles, can't you, Emma?" asked Lida.

Emma smiled and pursed up her lips, and out came the sound the robins make just before rain.

They turned in at Grandma Butler's place. Caddie and Lida sat down in the hammock under the pines to wait while Emma took the candle mold around to the back door.

"Oh, Emma," said Grandma Butler. "I'm so glad you've come by. I was just wondering what in the world I'd do. Johnny forgot to take the cow to pasture this morning before he left, and she's been bawling her head off ever since. I'd have taken her long ago, but my legs are full of rheumatics today. If you'll just drive her down for me, Johnny will see that she gets home tonight."

Emma thought of telling Grandma Butler that she was on her way to Eau Galle to see Dr. Hearty's wonderful Medicine Show, but she didn't like to disappoint people and she could hear the cow bawling mournfully in the barn. It wouldn't take long, and if she hurried she could catch the girls before they got to the crossroads. She ran around the house and told them to walk kind of slow and she would catch them up as soon as she could. Then, with the basket of eggs on one arm and a stick in the other hand, Emma drove the old cow down to the pasture.

The cow took her time about getting there and kept stopping every few steps to eat by the way, but finally she was safe behind pasture bars and Emma could hurry once more. She crawled under the pasture fence and skirted the swampy place behind Butler's farm. A red-winged blackbird, swaying on a reed, gave a fluty call and Emma whistled back at him. She was used to swampland and the birds that lived there. She took a short cut across fields, and she could see Caddie and Lida on the road ahead of her.

When she came to the crossroads, they were still ahead of her.

They waved and called, "Hurry up, Emma!"

"You go on. I'll catch up with you," called Emma.

But she was beginning to wonder if she would, for she would have to take the other branch of the crossroad for nearly a quarter of a mile to go by the blacksmith's house. Of course there was a lane there that made a short cut back to the main road to Eau Galle, and if she hurried she might catch them before they came into town.

She ran into the crossroads store with her basket of eggs. Both Mr. Hooper and his brother were busy attending to customers and Emma had to wait. She tapped her toe impatiently on the floor. The three little Hooper boys were playing tag around the cracker and gingersnap barrels, but they stopped and came to stand and stare at Emma.

"You goin' to the Medicine Show to Eau Galle?"

"I aim to," said Emma, smiling. "Are you?"

"Pa won't let us," they said dismally. "We

ain't never seen a show like that with torch-light and magic and banjo singin'."

"I never have either," said Emma. "I'm real pleased to get away to go."

Mr. Hooper took her basket now and began counting the eggs with great deliberation.

"Mis' McCantry want any groceries?"

"No. You're to credit the eggs to her account, please."

"Which way you going?"

"I'm going by the blacksmith's house to borrow a quilt pattern and then by the lane into Eau Galle."

"Fine!" said Mr. Hooper. "You're just the person I'm looking for. There's a letter here come for Mr. Tatum, and you can drop it by for the old man without going fifty steps out of your way. I'd send the little boys, but the last time they took a letter to him they dropped it in the mud and he couldn't half read it. Now he won't have them on the place. But I know you're always careful, Emma."

"Yes, sir," said Emma.

She wasn't surprised because, ever since the family had come back and settled on the corner of the Woodlawn and Nightingale places, people had trusted her with their errands. Somehow they never trusted her mother or Pearly, but they always trusted Emma. It was not very convenient if one were in a hurry. She stuck the letter in her pocket and hurried faster than ever.

It was considerably more than fifty steps out of her way to Mr. Tatum's door, but perhaps Mr. Hooper had forgotten. The old man was a long time answering her knock and, when he came, he looked as if he had been sleeping.

"Letter, eh?" he said, peering at it short-sightedly. "You'll have to come in and read it to me, my dear. I've broken my spectacles."

Emma sighed. This was beginning to assume the proportions of a bad dream—one of those dreams in which you try so hard to get somewhere on time and everything conspires to stop you. She stepped inside the door and broke the seal of the letter. How untidy Mr. Tatum's kitchen was! There were dirty pans and dishes in the sink, and the floor couldn't have been swept for days. If only she hadn't been in such a hurry—

"It's from your daughter, Hazel," said Emma. "She says she'll be up by the steamer on Thursday afternoon."

"Thursday?" said the old man. "Ain't that today?"

Emma thought. Yes, the girls had said, "Ask your mother to let you off *Thursday* afternoon, because there's going to be a medicine show in Eau Galle."

"That's right," said Emma. "It's today. The steamer ought to get in any time now."

"My land!" said Mr. Tatum. "Look at this house, and Hazel neat as a pin! But I've had lumbago in my back for nearly a week."

"You tell me what to do," said Emma. "I'm a mighty hand at tidying."

She flew around the way she had to do at home on a Saturday morning. While the kettle boiled she swept the floor, and when the water was hot she clattered through the dishes and pans. Mr. Tatum straightened up the beds and picked up the old newspapers which he had left lying on the front-room floor. The house began to look better.

"What you got to eat?" asked Emma.

"Ham an' potatoes," said Mr. Tatum doubtfully.

"Anything in the garden?"

"Rhubarb. But I ain't pulled it for a long time on account of my back."

"Rhubarb sauce an' hot biscuits," said Emma to herself.

She ran out into the garden and found the rhubarb. It was rather old now but it would do. The sun was getting low in the sky; almost any moment Mr. Tatum's daughter might come walking up the path. She washed the rhubarb and cut it up and put it on in a saucepan with a little water. Mr. Tatum peeled the potatoes and sliced the ham while she mixed up the biscuits. When the rhubarb began to bubble and turn soft and pink, she added the sugar to it and took it off to cool.

"Now you put the biscuits in the oven as soon as you start the ham, and you'll have a real nice supper for her."

"Won't you stay an' eat, Emma?"

"No, I'm in a kind of a hurry," said Emma. "Thanks just the same."

She ran down the road to the blacksmith's house. The sun was going lower. Cowbells tinkled across the fields. A catbird called and, without stopping to think, Emma answered it.

"Mis' Peavy, Mama wants to know please can she borrow your Star of Bethlehem quilt pattern?"

"Why, yes, Emma, if she'll think to return it."

"*I'll* remember," Emma said.

"It may take me a minute to hunt it up. Will you hold the baby for me while I look?"

"Yes, ma'am," said Emma.

She sat in the big rocker and held the baby. It was the first time she had sat down since morning, and it made her realize that she was tired. The blacksmith's wife was taking a long time to find the quilt pattern, but it didn't matter now. Emma knew that she was too late. Supper would be over at Lida's Grandma's before she could get to Eau Galle. She might still be in time to see the Medicine Show; but it would soon be getting dark, and if she should miss the girls in the crowd she would have no way of getting home again that night. She tried to think back over the afternoon and wonder if she could have hurried a little more here or there. But it didn't seem as if she would have done anything differently, even if she could. An unexpected tear rolled down the side of Emma's nose, but she brushed it hastily away. The Peavy baby was warm and soft to hold, and he was going to sleep in her arms.

When she left the Peavys' farm with the quilt pattern in her pocket, the sun had just slipped below the horizon and the sky was all clear and softly green like glass. There were two tiny pink clouds overhead, and the first star was just beginning to wink experimentally.

Down the road ahead of her Emma saw something which had not been there when she came by before. It was an odd-looking red wagon—almost like a little house on wheels, and something seemed to have gone wrong with it. One of the wheels was sunk in a muddy rut of the road, and a man in a stove-pipe hat was out examining the extent of the damage.

Emma came up alongside and looked on.

"I guess you broke your axle, mister."

"Snakes an' fishes!" said the man. "I guess I did!"

A little spotted dog jumped out of the wagon and came to bark at Emma. A fat spotted horse craned its neck around and rolled its eyes to see why the wagon wouldn't budge. There were gold filigree designs around the top of the red caravan, and iron sockets that looked as if they might be made for holding torches. The man wore a long frock coat and a marvelous flowered waistcoat. It was all very strange. Emma's heart began to beat more quickly.

"Trouble, trouble all day long!" said the man. "I never see the like. First the mare throws a shoe and I have to wait to get her reshod. Then the sheriff wants to see my license and I've got to go five miles out of my way—and now this! I'll never get to Eau Galle in time for the show."

"Why, that's just the way it's been with

me!" said Emma in surprise. "I started out real early this afternoon; but somebody stopped me every way I turned, and I'll never get to Eau Galle in time for the show."

"Then we're in the same boat, sister," said the big man, smiling. His troubles really seemed to sit upon him very lightly. "Do you know where there's a blacksmith?"

"Yes, I just come from his house. His shop's down to the crossroads—not far."

He opened the back of the red van, and Emma saw that it was lined with racks full of bottles. Suddenly her heart stood still, and then it began to pound at double its usual rate. She went around to the side of the wagon to make sure. Yes, it was there in red and gold letters.

### DR. HEARTY'S MARVELOUS CURE-ALL

"But . . . but . . ." said Emma breathlessly. "You *are* the show."

"At your service, ma'am," said Dr. Hearty cheerfully. He had taken a long pole out of the wagon and now he began to rig up a crude sort of lever for hoisting the wheel out of the rut. "You take the horse's bridle—will you, sister?—and get him to move along right smart when I give you the word."

"Yes, sir," said Emma, trotting to the horse's head.

Her thoughts were in a turmoil. Why, there wouldn't be any show in Eau Galle to-night! Dr. Hearty was here—in the road—no farther along than Emma McCantry.

Emma and Dr. Hearty coaxed and lifted and prodded and groaned for nearly half an hour before they got the horse and the disabled caravan as far as the crossroads and the blacksmith's shop. But they were both cheerful about it.

Dr. Hearty seemed to accept everything that came along as pleasantness, and to Emma this was real adventure. A barn swallow flew over and Emma couldn't help imitating its eerie cry.

"Can you do more of those?" asked Dr. Hearty curiously.

"About ten, I guess," said Emma carelessly.

There were usually quite a few people around the crossroads on a fine evening, but most of them had gone into Eau Galle tonight to see the Medicine Show. Those who remained were people who wished they might go but were prevented from doing so, such as the little Hooper boys and old man Toomey, with the wooden leg, and the men who had to tend shop or forge. These remaining few came out and stood about the caravan in openmouthed amazement.

The sight of even so small a crowd made Dr. Hearty's eyes sparkle. While the blacksmith went to work on the broken axle, Dr. Hearty began to make a speech.

"La-*dees* and *Gent*lemen," he said, "if you cannot go to Dr. Hearty's highly educating and entertaining display of music, art, and magic, Dr. Hearty will come to you."

He took out a worn old banjo and began such a lively tune that the little Hooper boys could not resist jigging and doing handsprings all over the grass. When the jig was finished, Dr. Hearty struck more plaintive chords and raised his rich bass voice in a sad ballad, "Dying at the Door."

"Through the dark streets I am wand'-
        ring alone,
    Bowed down and weary with hope over-
        thrown;
    Seeking from torturing memory rest,
    Trying to stifle the pain at my breast.
    Stained tho' I am, yet on this cruel night
    I'm seeking again my old home's fire-
        light.

Oh, you who once loved me, forgive, I
   implore;
Oh, pity me tonight, for I'm dying at
   your door.
Have pity tonight for I'm dying, at your
   door.


"Weary, sighing, hopeless, dying,
What a change from days of yore.
Father, mother, husband, children,
I am dying at your door."


Emma couldn't help wiping her eyes on the
corner of her apron. The mouths of the little
Hooper boys had gone down at the corners.
In fact Dr. Hearty's audience was almost in
tears over the sad fate of the heroine of the
ballad, when he stopped singing as suddenly
as he had begun.

"Pardon me, miss, but you've a half dollar
sticking out of your ear."

Emma was perfectly amazed to have Dr.
Hearty reach out and pluck a half dollar quite
painlessly out of her ear. It was a very nimble
half dollar indeed; for after it had disappeared
under a silk handkerchief, it suddenly popped
up again in old man Toomey's beard, was
once more lost in Dr. Hearty's stovepipe hat,

and finally came to light in the youngest Hooper boy's pocket.

"And now," said Dr. Hearty, "a little local talent, my friends. My able assistant, Miss Emma, will now favor us with her bird-call imitations."

Emma was as much astonished as when Dr. Hearty found a half dollar in her ear, but she wasn't frightened.

"This is the robin's early-morning song," she said, pursing up her lips. "This is the bobolink.... This is the redwing...."

When she had finished they all applauded. Even the blacksmith stopped working on the axle to clap his hands, and Emma found herself making a curtsy just like a regular actor.

"And now, again, my friends," said Dr. Hearty, "to demonstrate to you the salubrious properties of my Marvelous Cure-All, I should like you to witness its remarkable effect on a poor old man."

In a moment the spotted dog, dressed in a small pair of trousers, with spectacles on his nose, came walking around the caravan on his hind legs. He appeared to be in great distress and presently lay down as if at death's door. Dr. Hearty felt his pulse and asked him various questions concerning his health, to which the little dog replied with barks and dismal whines. When all seemed lost, a sip of Dr. Hearty's Cure-All miraculously restored him to health and vivacity—to the extreme delight of Emma and the little boys.

"I'd like a bottle of that myself," said Mr. Hooper. "Have you et, Dr. Hearty?"

"No," said Dr. Hearty, "but I'd admire to do so. Will you trade me some supper for a bottle of Cure-All?"

"Step right over to the store, doctor, an' we'll do business."

"My able assistant is also unfed," said the doctor.

"That's all right," said Mr. Hooper. "Come right in, Emma. I'll feed ye both."

The store was mellow with lamplight. Emma sat on a cracker barrel and Dr. Hearty leaned on a counter beside her. Crackers and cheese had never tasted finer. It was a rare meal and spiced with magic, for Dr. Hearty seemed as clever at extracting crackers from people's ears as he had been with half dollars. Crackers came out of the lamp chimney and disappeared mysteriously into flour sacks, and gingersnaps materialized out of thin air.

It was a lovely evening, full of adventure. But at last the axle was mended and Emma knew that she must be on her way home.

"Come in to Eau Galle tomorrow, Emma," said Dr. Hearty, "and I'll let you do your bird imitations for all the people."

Emma smiled and shook her head.

"My mother couldn't spare me off another day, I guess."

"Well, anyway, here's a parting gift," said the doctor, "and thank you kindly for helping me get out of the mudhole."

He held out a shiny new bottle of Dr. Hearty's Marvelous Cure-All.

Emma took it with reverence and awe.

"I don't seem to need much medicine," she said, "but I'll always keep it just like this to remember you by."

It was cool and fresh walking home in the starlight with so many things to think about and the wonderful bottle clutched under her arm.

When she was almost at the little lane that turned down between the Woodlawns' and the Nightingales' places, she heard Mr. Woodlawn's wagon come rattling along behind her.

"Oh, Emma, whatever happened to you?" cried the girls. "But it's just as well you didn't come. What do you think? There wasn't any show at all!"

"Do tell!" said Emma, turning in at the

lane. "I'm really sorry that you didn't get to see the show!"

Behind the barn a whippoorwill gave out its wistful cry, and Emma answered it.

# 7

## The Circuit Rider's Story

*"Cast thy bread upon the waters: for thou shalt find it after many days,"* said Mr. Tanner. "Put your faith in prayer. The Lord will provide."

Mr. Tanner was not in church; he was not preaching a sermon. But, having delivered himself of three good texts, he stretched his long legs toward the Woodlawns' fire and prepared to tell a story.

"I was brought up on those three texts," Mr. Tanner continued. "You see, my father was a circuit rider before me. There were a passel of us young ones, and we grew up in the worst kind of poverty; but when we thought that we should have to go to bed

hungry for lack of food to put in our mouths,
the Lord was always sure to provide."

Warren looked at Mr. Tanner's brown,
rugged face and asked timidly, "Could you see
Him? Did He come Himself?"

It was not a strange question, for Mr. Tanner made heaven seem close and eternal punishment yawn as near by as the root cellar. He
made the Lord seem a friendly person who
might walk in at any moment with loaves and
fishes in His hands.

"How would you answer that one, Mr.
Ward?" inquired the circuit rider.

Mr. Ward was a pale, slender young man
with a diffident smile. The Woodlawns all
looked at him now to see what he would say.
For Mr. Ward was to be the new preacher, the
one who would live in Dunnville in a house
of his own all the year round instead of riding
the circuit. Tomorrow he would preach his
first sermon in the schoolhouse, and after that
the people of the town were planning to
build him a church with lumber from the
mill at Eau Galle. It was a sign that the town
was growing. When they had a church of their
own and a regular preacher instead of a circuit rider, it meant that pioneer days were
almost over.

Mr. Ward had said very little that evening,

but now he answered Warren's question about the Lord.

"I don't guess Mr. Tanner saw the Lord Himself. God has mysterious ways of making provision for those who love Him. He has all kinds of messengers."

"I will tell you a story," said Mr. Tanner.

Tom and Caddie and Warren moved closer to the fire and to Mr. Tanner's long legs. It was not so much to be near the warmth of the fire on the first chilly evening of autumn as it was to be near the source of the story. They did not want to miss a word. Stories were as rare and delightful as apples or peppermint candy.

"As I was saying just now, my father was a circuit rider like myself. His circuit was back East in a section that's pretty well civilized now. But in those days it was as much a frontier as Wisconsin has been since I came here."

"Were there Indians there?" Caddie asked.

"Yes, there were, Caroline Augusta," said Mr. Tanner. "If you'll just be patient, I'll come to the Indians as soon as possible."

The children breathed a sigh of contentment, and Warren hitched his stool a trifle closer until his chin almost rested on Mr. Tanner's knee.

"My father had a little homestead in the

woods with a log cabin on it where we children lived with our mother the year round
while Father was away riding his circuit and
bringing the word of God to distant settlements. I could tell you more than one story
about our struggles there: how we boys did
man's work before we were in our teens; how
hostile Indians came, threatening to burn us
out; and how my mother kept them at bay
with Father's old blunderbuss, although she
hadn't an ounce of ammunition for it. She
deceived those savages, but it was a deception
which I have always felt the Lord forgave her.
Yes, I could tell you of a dozen instances
when we were on the point of starvation; but
I'll tell you just one, to answer Warren's question about how the Lord provides."

Mr. Tanner paused and cleared his throat,
and Father took that opportunity to put another chunk of wood upon the fire, for it
looked as if the story might outlast the sticks
which were already blazing.

"But why should you be near starvation,
Mr. Tanner?" Tom asked. "Didn't you have
good crops? Didn't they pay your father anything?"

"Maybe you don't know what a circuit rider's life is like, Tom. He has no fixed salary.
People give him what they think he's worth,

and if the folks in one settlement feel poor
that year, they say, 'Oh, well, the folks at the
next settlement up the river will pay him. It's
no concern of ours.' And maybe the folks up
the river say, 'He probably got paid at the last
place downriver. It's not *our* responsibility.'
No, a circuit rider's life is not all as pleasant
as a Saturday evening at the Woodlawns'. As
to our crops, it was my mother and us six little children who had to hew a farm out of the
wilderness while my father was away preaching God's word. Maybe you see now why the
Lord himself sometimes had to look after us."

"I guess I do," said Tom.

"Tell about the Indians," urged Hetty, a
little tired already of all this talk about a
preacher's livelihood.

"Well, we had more trouble with our Indians than you have had here. Even your mas-
sacre scare was nothing to some of the things
we went through. But the trouble lay not so
much with the Indians themselves as with a
few of the white men who had brought Satan
with them into the wilderness instead of the
Lord God."

Warren was opening his mouth to ask if
Mr. Tanner had seen Satan, but the circuit
rider went right on speaking without giving
him an opportunity.

"Most of these renegade whites were fur traders; and instead of giving the Indians honest goods in exchange for their furs, they gave them liquor—'firewater,' the Indians called it. It was a shameful but a not uncommon sight to see a drunken Indian staggering along a forest trail or through the streets of one of the settlements. Fired by strong drink, the savage nature of the Indian broke forth and he was likely to commit any crime or folly. For that reason we very greatly feared the Indians in our region.

"Now one cold winter evening, with snow lying white on the icy ground, it happened that my father was riding home through the forest after an absence of several months. On the way he fell in with a settler of the neighborhood, and they were both glad of the company, for men did not ride abroad much after dark. Ordinarily my father would have stopped before dark at a settler's cabin, but being so near his own home, he continued on. The two men had to pass near an Indian encampment on the way, and the settler was afraid and wished to go the long way round.

"'No,' my father said. 'If you are afraid, pray. When you have cast your troubles on the Lord, you will have no fear.'

"Well, no doubt they prayed well, for they

passed through the Indian encampment without fear and without difficulty, the Indians only looking at them with dark, forbidding faces.

" 'My friend, you see how easy it becomes,' said my father.

" 'Right you are, Parson,' replied the farmer, 'but I wouldn't go back through that Indian camp again for a hogshead of salt pork and a dozen sugar loaves.'

"They rode on in silence for perhaps a mile, their horses sometimes floundering in deep snow, sometimes slipping on bare ice. The breath of their mouths whitened the dark air like smoke.

" 'A man would soon freeze on a night like this, did he not keep moving,' said the settler over his shoulder, for he was riding ahead.

" 'Aye, you are right,' said my father.

"As he spoke, the settler's horse suddenly shied at something dark which lay beside the trail.

"The man rode hurriedly by, calling back to my father, 'Take care! There's a dead Indian by the wayside.'

" 'Dead?' said my father. 'How do you know?'

"He drew in his horse's bridle rein and prepared to dismount.

" 'In God's name, Parson Tanner, you're not going to get down off your horse on a night like this for a dirty Indian, are you? He may be lying in wait to stab you or, if he is dead, the other savages may find you with him and kill you too.'

"But my father got down and tethered his horse, saying to himself, *'They looked on him, and passed by on the other side. But a certain Samaritan, as he journeyed, came where he was: and when he saw him he had compassion on him. . . .'*

" 'I don't know what you are mumbling, Parson,' said the settler, 'but I beg you not to stop now in these woods on such a night.'

"Still my father would not be dissuaded. He knelt beside the Indian and found that he was still breathing, but that he was in a drunken stupor from the white man's fire-water. Another half-hour lying in that bitter cold and he would freeze to death, nor ever wake again in this world.

" 'There is only one thing to do,' said my father, 'and that is to lift him up before me on my saddle and carry him back to the encampment, where his friends can look out for him.'

" 'Parson!' cried the settler. 'And you so mad against strong drink! Leave the fellow, I tell you. 'Twill be one less bad Indian.'

" 'Come here,' said my father, 'and give me a hand with him.'

"Well, grumbling all the way, the farmer came back and helped my father lift the unconscious savage and lay him across my father's saddle, and back they went the long dark way to the unfriendly encampment.

"The Indians looked at my father in astonishment as he rode among them again; but when they realized that he had saved one of their number from death, their scowling faces grew less hostile.

"It was late that night when my father reached our cabin. But we children heard him and came helter-skelter out of our makeshift beds.

" 'Pap, have you brought us something to eat?'

" 'The sorghum and salt are used up, Pappy, and there's only a few handfuls of meal. Mother said you'd bring it all with you when you came, and money for new shoes too.'

"My father sat down by the table, and he looked played out with his long journey.

" 'Get back to your beds, young ones,' Mother said. 'Can't you see he's tired out?'

"I think already she must have known what we found out the next day, that his pockets were as empty as when he had left us in the early fall.

"Well, it's hard to go hungry and without shoes in the wintertime. In summer you don't need shoes and there are berries and nuts and wild plums in the woods even if the crops are poor. But winter is a bitter time. My poor father was not even a very good hunter and game was scarce that year. Later we boys grew into mighty hunters, as clever to stalk a deer and catch him with an arrow to his heart as any Indian lad. But that winter we were little fellows and the cold and hunger bit into us.

"That winter for the first and the last time I heard my mother question my father's way of life.

" 'It's not right, Tanner,' she said. 'It's not right for the Lord to come before a man's family. If you weren't off doing the Lord's business instead of staying at home and attending to your own, your little children would have food in their mouths and shoes on their feet and decent clothes on their backs. And all these people you go and preach to, do they care enough about you to put two bits into the collection plate? No, indeed! Oh, Parson Tanner is a right good exhorter no doubt, but when it comes to paying him anything, let someone else do it. The Lord will provide!'

"My mother said it with bitter sarcasm in her voice.

"My father continued to sit by the empty table, looking very stern and pale, his eyes resting on the floor.

" 'Yes, Elsa,' he said in his quiet voice, 'I still believe it. The Lord will look after His own.'

"It went on so for a few days more, and we were all hungry and crying and at odds with one another. My mother had made some thin gruel—which satisfied none of us—out of the last of the meal and, after we had eaten it, she stood in front of our father with her hands on her hips.

" 'And now what?' says she. 'Don't tell me again that the Lord will provide!'

"I had never seen my father angry before then. Something like blue lightning flashed out of his eyes.

" 'Elsa,' he said, 'You've made too free with the Lord's name of late. Get down on your knees, all of you! I'm going to pray.'

"We didn't hesitate a minute. Even my mother got down awkwardly onto her knees, wiping her eyes with the corner of her apron.

" 'Oh, Lord God,' my father prayed, 'there are so many other people in this world who need Thy help that it seems kind of selfish to call Thy attention to us. But we're here in the wilderness alone, and it's been a hard winter. Oh, Almighty Lord, forgive us if we beseech Thee to look down upon us here and see our necessity. Forgive us if we have faltered in our faith in Thee. O Lord, provide for us in some way until spring comes and we can provide for ourselves. *Amen.*'

"Whether from weakness or from some inner realization of the majesty of that moment, we all stayed on our knees after he had ceased praying. And while we were still kneeling there, we heard a horse's hoofs coming along the hard frozen track into the clearing. We children were suddenly frightened. Not one of us moved except Mother, who turned her head with a strange look of expectancy in her eyes.

"The horse's hoofs stopped at the door and there was a shuffling of moccasined feet in the entryway. I felt my hair prickle on top of my head where my scalp lock grew. Still not one of us moved.

"The latch clicked off the hasp, and the door was thrust open and banged back against the wall. An Indian stalked in. On his shoulder he had a haunch of venison, which he flung down upon the bare table. He fumbled an instant in a little buckskin pouch he wore at his belt and brought out a small round yellow piece, which he clinked down beside the fresh meat. Our father rose like a person in a dream.

"'You're the man I found lying in the woods that night,' he said, as if he were talking to himself.

"'White fella good man,' the Indian said gravely. 'Me give 'um gift.'

"At that he turned and stalked out, mounted his pony, and rode away among the trees. We cried our thanks after him, but our voices only echoed in the empty woods. We never saw him again."

A little silence fell as Mr. Tanner ceased speaking.

At last Mrs. Woodlawn broke it by saying, "Mr. Tanner, after such a childhood, I am amazed that you yourself should have become a circuit rider, knowing what the life was like."

The big preacher smiled at his hostess.

"Ma'am," he said, "that's the very best kind of childhood for a traveling preacher to have. It conditions him early. There's only one way in which I differ from my father—I've never asked a woman to share my wandering life with me, and I'll never have a child of my own to run in the cold woods without shoes."

"But now that the country's getting settled

so that permanent churches can be built, why don't you settle down with it?"

"Me?" said Mr. Tanner. "No, I'll leave the settling to Mr. Ward."

He laughed his big comfortable laugh, and in his eyes they saw the look of forest places farther West where trails were just beginning to be blazed.

But the children wanted to return to the story.

Hetty pulled at Mr. Tanner's sleeve and asked, "What was the yellow thing he took out of his pouch that clinked?"

"A five-dollar gold piece," said Mr. Tanner. "Five dollars went a long way in those days. It bought us meal and sorghum and salt pork to tide us over until spring."

"How did an Indian happen onto a five-dollar gold piece?" wondered Tom.

"I don't know," said Mr. Tanner. "We accepted it. We weren't in a mood to question. Besides, you know, there's an old saying: *Never look a gift horse in the mouth.*"

"Especially when it's from the Lord," said Warren reverently.

# 8

## "Go, My Son, into the Forest" or What Warren Did About It

It was not easy to forget Mr. Tanner's story. It made the children realize the difficulties of a frontier preacher's life, and it lent a kind of glamour of adventurous sanctity even to young Mr. Jedediah Ward, who had come to be the pastor at Dunnville.

Mr. Ward was a nice young man and a very pleasant preacher. If he did not roar and rave against the sins of the earth in a mighty voice as Mr. Tanner did, he made the golden streets and harps of heaven seem sweeter; and his fine tenor voice added much to the singing of the hymns.

He stayed for a few days with the Woodlawns until the ladies of the congregation had
furnished out the little cabin in Dunnville
which had been built for him by the men.
When it was finished he moved into it, and
spread his books and papers all about, and
began to cook his own meals. Then the men
who had built his cabin started the mightier
building of his church.

Mr. Ward was still young enough to arouse
Mrs. Woodlawn's motherly kindness.

She saw his paleness and his thinness and
she said aloud, with a great sigh of sympathy,
"That poor, dear young man. I declare to
goodness he looks half starved!"

"He just hasn't filled out yet," Father said.
"He's like a young tree; he's been too busy
shooting up to send out branches."

"No," Mother said firmly. "I am sure he's
but half fed. We'll have him here to dinner of
a Sunday, anyway. It's the least that we can do
for him."

*The least that they could do!* The children
thought this over as they walked to school.
Hetty and Minnie had run on ahead; but
Tom, Caddie, and Warren walked more
slowly, discussing weighty matters.

"Mr. Tanner is so big and healthy and
brown," Caddie said, "and look what *he*

suffered when *he* was young. Mr. Ward's childhood days must have been sumpin terrible."

"What worries me," Tom said, "Father doesn't seem to take it very seriously. I wonder if he's doing all he should for Mr. Ward?"

"How do you mean?" asked Warren, his face puckered with anxiety.

"Well, you know what Mr. Tanner said about folks up the river leaving it to the folks downriver to take care of the preacher; and the folks downriver saying that the ones upriver would take care of him, so why should they worry—"

"But Dunnville folks have turned out to build and furnish him a house," said Caddie. "Mother and Father gave a bedstead and two chairs, and Father loaned them his team to pull stumps and grade for the new church."

"Sure," Tom said. "I guess they've done what they could all right. But I was thinking—we haven't done anything."

The three walked in silence for a few paces. Tom's words and the memory of the circuit rider's story filled them with a sense of guilt. There were two kinds of sins, they knew—sins of commission and sins of omission. Just at the moment they couldn't remember any sins which they had *committed*. (There might

very well be some, but so far even Hetty had
not discovered them.) But if it came to thinking of things which they had *omitted* doing
when they should have done them, then perhaps they had sinned against poor Mr. Ward.

Caddie said, "Well, I've got my wool
money. If I gave a tenth of that, that would be
a tithe. Wouldn't it? That's what the Bible
says you ought to give."

Her voice sounded relieved. That was a
simple way of getting Mr. Jedediah Ward off
her conscience.

"I've got those horseshoes I've picked up on
the roads," Tom said. "I can sell them to the
blacksmith and put the money in the collection plate."

"What can I do?" asked Warren bleakly.

Nobody answered him, for they had
reached the schoolyard by that time. Tom saw
two of the older boys skinning the cat on the
high bar between two pine trees on which the
little children's swing was strung, and with a
yell like a wild Indian's, he went to match his
prowess to theirs. At the same time Maggie
Bunn and Jane Flusher darted out and en-
folded Caddie into one of those whispering,
giggling, three-girl secret societies which the
boys abhorred.

Warren stood all alone by the schoolhouse

door, and he felt very sad indeed. Caddie had her wool money. Tom had been picking up horseshoes for years. But Warren's pocket, like the pocket of a preacher, was always empty. Coins often entered his pocket, it is true; but they never lingered there. They passed out very rapidly to more delightful places. They rolled away to the candy counter at the Dunnville store; they hurried off after tops and marbles and kites. When the candy was eaten, the tops and marbles lost, and the kites blown far away across the woods and prairies to the amazement of the eagles and the Indians, Warren had nothing left in his pockets but his hands.

He felt very sorry and ashamed. Here was poor Mr. Ward, half starved, Mother said, and Warren was like the heartless people in Mr. Tanner's tale: he gave the preacher nothing.

School took up as usual with roll call and singing of the multiplication tables. Then while the little children on the front benches braided mats, Miss Parker assembled the older children for a reading lesson. Instead of their McGuffey Readers, for a week now Miss Parker had had them read a story about Indians. It was really a long poem written by the Massachusetts poet Mr. Longfellow, and it

told about an Indian boy named Hiawatha
and all his friends in the forest. Usually Warren was very much interested, although he did
have a hard time with the long names and he
thought it would have been easier if Mr.
Longfellow had just gone ahead and told the
story, as Mr. Tanner told his, without stopping to put in all the hard words.

But today Warren was so busy wondering
what he could give to poor Mr. Ward that he
did not listen to the story of Hiawatha.
Dimly, through the fog of his worry, he heard
the various readers taking up the tale where
they had left it yesterday. He should have
been warned when Caddie began to read, for
she sat across the aisle from him. Her voice
went tripping lightly and gaily among the
forests of long words.

"'Minne-wawa!' said the pine-trees,
    'Mudway-aushka!' said the water.
    Saw the firefly, Wah-wah-taysee. . . .'"

Caddie was the best speller in the class, and
she enjoyed the long words very much. She
would have gone right on reading as long as
anyone would listen to her. But unfortunately
Miss Parker's sharp eyes were fixed on Warren's vacant ones.

"Just a moment, Caddie," she said, holding up her hand. "There is one person in this class who is not paying strict attention. Warren, will you kindly tell me what Caddie has been reading?"

*"Wah-wah-wah . . ."* said Warren, trying to remember.

*"Taysee,"* whispered Caddie under her breath.

*"Wah-wah-wah . . ."* repeated Warren distractedly.

"Pass him the book, Caddie," said Miss Parker. "Let him find the passage for himself."

Caddie couldn't help feeling sorry for Warren. He really should have been paying attention, especially when she had just been reading so beautifully; but still she knew how difficult it was for him to have to stand up and read in public. As she passed him the book she put her thumb on the line where he should start.

Warren was smart enough to begin reading where her thumb had been, but the sight of the long words paralyzed his tongue.

" 'Minnie-Minnie-Minnie . . .' "

"Present," piped little Minnie from the front row, thinking that the roll was being called a second time.

" '*Minne-wawa*,' Warren," prompted Miss Parker ominously.

" '*Minne-haha!' said the pine trees*," read Warren hastily. " '*Muddy Oshkosh!' said the water*."

"No, no, Warren," corrected Miss Parker. "Oshkosh is in the geography lesson."

"*Saw the firefly, Wah-wah-wah-wah . . .*"

"You may be seated," said Miss Parker coldly. "It is clear that you were not paying attention to the reading of a beautiful poem, Warren. You may stay after school and read it aloud to me, when we shall have more time to go into the fine points of spelling and pronunciation."

Warren sighed. One trouble often led right into another one, Warren knew from experience, and this seemed no exception to the rule.

Sitting on the high stool beside Miss Parker's desk after school, Warren reflected sadly that surely Mr. Longfellow, who was called the children's poet, did not intend to have little children staying after school because of him. If only Mr. Longfellow had been a trifle more considerate in the matter of long, queer words!

At last Miss Parker finished correcting the

arithmetic slates and turned around in her seat to look at Warren.

"Whatever was the matter with you this morning, Warren? *Wah-wah-wah!* You sounded like a frog who has swallowed too large a minnow."

Warren gulped.

"I'm sorry, ma'am. I'll try to do better."

"I know," Miss Parker said more kindly, "that some of the words are hard. That's why you have to pay attention, you see. But when we get on a little farther you will like the poem better, I am sure, and there won't be so many difficult words. I was going to make you write *Mudwayaushka* fifty times on the blackboard, Warren, but now I've changed my mind."

"You have, ma'am?" asked Warren hopefully.

He could still catch up with Tom and Caddie before they reached home if he ran like the wind. But her next words dashed his hopes.

"Yes, instead of that I'm going to let you read ahead a little bit. Begin here, where my finger is pointing."

Warren sighed heavily. It was surely a disappointing day, but there was nothing for it but to read where Teacher pointed.

"Then Iagoo, the great boaster . . .
　Made a bow for Hiawatha;
　From a branch of ash he made it,
　From an oak-bough made the arrows,
　Tipped with flint, and winged with
　　feathers,
　And the cord he made of deer-skin."

Well, this was a little better! Warren's voice began to lose its singsong drone.

"Then he said to Hiawatha:
　'Go, my son, into the forest,
　Where the red deer herd together,
　Kill for us a famous roebuck,
　Kill for us a deer with antlers!' "

All the way home, walking by himself after the others had dispersed, Warren heard words singing in his ears.

"Go, my son, into the forest,
　Kill for us a deer with antlers."

Something else, which he had lately heard, echoed in his mind. It was Mr. Tanner's great voice saying, "We boys grew into mighty hunters, as clever to stalk a deer and catch him with an arrow to his heart as any Indian lad."

Suddenly Warren jumped up in the air and cracked his heels together. Betweem them, Mr. Tanner and the children's poet had solved his problem for him.

On Saturday morning, very early before anyone else was up, Warren arose and quietly pulled on his clothes. He did not bother to wash his face. Washing the face seemed to him an unnecessary refinement which was only visited upon boys with mothers and sisters. This morning he had no time for it. He went to the kitchen and lifted down from the pegs behind the door Father's handsome spring-lock gun. Father had taught him how to shoot it, but he had never before taken it out alone.

Now Warren shivered a little in the frosty autumn dawn as he went across the fields carrying Father's gun. His mind wrestled with the thought of how he could carry home a famous roebuck if he were fortunate enough to get one. Hiawatha or the Tanner boys would have slung it carelessly over one shoulder, but he thought that he should probably be obliged to fetch Robert Ireton from the barn to help him. Of course, he could always call on Tom and Caddie to drag the deer with antlers home, but they would want to know why he had not taken them with him in the first place and what he intended to do with the prize now that he had it.

The truth of the matter was that Warren did not himself quite know why he was keeping his expedition a secret from the family. It was perhaps because Caddie had her wool money, and Tom had his horseshoes, and Warren had only empty pockets. When he flung down the haunch of venison on Mr. Ward's table, he wanted it to be his own contribution. The most truly generous persons are those who give silently without hope of praise or reward.

Roebucks did not seem to be plentiful in the woods about Dunnville that Saturday morning. The first large moving object which Warren glimpsed through the trees turned out to be Flushers' cow. He was just pulling the trigger of Father's gun when he recognized her, and fortunately he had presence of mind enough to jog the gun upward in the nick of time so that the shot went over her back into the trees beyond. The frosty silence of the morning was scattered into terrible reverberations. The sound of the gun frightened Warren as much as it did the cow, and it set the bluejays and crows to chattering and scolding and the woods to echoing.

"Oh, golly!" thought Warren. "What if I'd killed the Flushers' cow!"

One thing the boy Hiawatha had never had

to contend with was the neighbors' cow. Warren had to sit down on a stump for a moment to catch his breath. It was partly, of course, because he hadn't had his breakfast that his stomach felt so queer.

But presently he got up and went on again.

The animals had all come out and looked at Hiawatha and begged, "Do not shoot me, Hiawatha." But nothing like that happened in Dunnville. Either the spring-lock gun or Warren's determined appearance kept them from showing themselves. He wasted another shot on a large brown object, glimpsed through the trees, which turned out to be a rock. Warren began to be a little anxious about the amount of Father's ammunition which he was wasting. Also he was very hungry.

Perhaps, after all, his stomach was as important in its own way as Mr. Ward's was. He began to hear Mother's voice saying, "Poor, dear boy, he looks half starved!" and surely the words referred to him.

The sun was well up in the sky now, and Warren reflected that the corn-meal mush would be cold on the breakfast table at home and that the bacon would all be eaten. Everybody would be saying, "Where is Warren?"

It was at this point that Warren gave up the

chase and turned homeward. But such is the
strangeness of fate that, the moment he had
given up the hunt as utterly useless, he saw a
large plump rabbit sitting quietly under a
thorn-apple tree, making of itself a perfect
target. Warren raised Father's gun and fired;
and while a rabbit was certainly not as fine a
prize as a roebuck, it was very much easier to
carry home.

One might have thought that now Warren's troubles were over. He had shot a nice
piece of game as his contribution to the sup-
port of the new preacher. A few hours earlier
that had been the only thing he could think
of doing which would make him happy. But
now that he had succeeded in getting an excellent, plump rabbit, he found the rest of his
day beset with difficulties.

First of all, of course, everybody wanted to
know where he had been and why he was
cleaning Father's gun. He was reproved for
being late for breakfast and for having muddy
boots.

"Why? Why? Why?" asked everybody, and
it was very difficult to put them off and still be
strictly honest. He hid the rabbit in the barn,
and that at least made one less "Why?" For if
they had seen it the Woodlawns would have
been sure to ask, "Why can't we have it for

dinner?" and "Who are you going to give it to?"

Hetty might even have said, "Warren has a gir-rul!"

No, it seemed impossible to Warren to confess that he had shot it for the preacher. The preacher! Here was Warren's next difficulty. How was he going to give the rabbit to the preacher without suffering great embarrassment? Should he knock on Mr. Ward's door and say, "Mr. Ward, I have brought you a present?" Should he open the door and fling it down on the table and stalk silently out again? To do either one seemed to Warren worse than having to read aloud in school— worse even than having to speak a piece. If only he could put it on the collection plate tomorrow in church! But the idea of a dead rabbit on the collection plate was somehow quite impossible.

Finally a solution occurred to him. Perhaps it was like going out to shoot a roebuck and returning with a rabbit, but at any rate it would save a shy boy some embarrassment.

At dusk that evening Warren went to the barn and tied the front and hind legs of the rabbit securely together with a bit of twine. Then he set out across the fields to Dunnville. It was almost dark when he arrived, and not a living soul saw him when he hung the rabbit by its feet over Mr. Ward's doorknob.

Warren seemed to be at peace with the world on the bright Sabbath morning which followed. But he still kept somewhat to himself—walking piously ahead of the others to the church service, which was being held in the schoolhouse until the new church should be finished.

"Funny about Warren," Tom said to Caddie. "Where'd you s'pose he went yesterday morning?"

"I don't know, and he was late to supper."

"I know. He'd had out Father's gun, too, and he'd shot it, because I saw him cleaning it up good before he put it back on the pegs."

"Did you bring your horseshoe money for the collection plate, Tom?"

"Ya. Did you bring yours?"

"Yes. Say, I wonder about Warren. Could it be he went hunting to get some money for the collection plate?"

But watching him later in church, they saw that he let the collection plate pass without putting anything in. He did not look the least bit troubled.

After the preaching, Mr. Ward stood at the schoolhouse door to shake everyone's hand as they passed out.

Mrs. Woodlawn smiled at him approvingly. Somehow Mr. Ward already seemed less pale and hungry-looking than when he had first arrived in Dunnville.

"Mr. Ward," Mother said, "will you come home and take Sunday dinner with us today?"

Young Mr. Ward hesitated just an instant as between two very delightful prospects.

Then he said, "I thank you, Mrs. Woodlawn, but may I take dinner with you some other Sunday? It just so happens that this week the Lord has provided me with a very fine rabbit, which is simmering in the pot at home."

Caddie darted a look at Warren. His ears were red with embarrassment, but his face wore an expression of pride and contentment. All the way home he walked a couple of yards ahead of Caddie and Tom with his chest thrust out like a person of importance.

Tom was a little bit annoyed.

"Should we dip him in the lake, just to cool him off some?" he asked.

Caddie shook her head.

"No, Tom, I don't think we'd ought to," Caddie said seriously. "It isn't everyone who's smart enough to do the Lord's work for Him."

# 9

# Nero Plays Cupid

The Woodlawns had been having one of their
jolliest evenings all by themselves, and then,
for no good reason that Caddie could see at
all, the sleighing party from town had come
by and spoiled everything. The sleighing
party hadn't even come to the door—that was
the worst of it perhaps. It had simply taken
the short-cut road which Father left open for
the use of the neighbors through the southwest corner of the farm. The short cut saved
about a mile for anyone who wished to go
from Dunnville to the main highway leading
to Durand, and Father was glad to have the
settlers use it when they were hauling logs or

grain. At night the bars were always put up on the gate, and the short-cut road was never used except in case of an emergency. But tonight the sleighing party used it.

It was a Saturday night, with no school the next day, and the Woodlawn children were allowed the Saturday-night privilege of staying up an hour or two later than usual. As soon as the supper things were cleared away, Mother had sat down at the melodeon, and Father and the children had all stood or sat around her to sing.

Sometimes Caddie thought that the Saturday-night "sings" were the finest moments in the week. Mother sang alto, and Father and Warren tenor. Tom was working hard on an uncertain bass which sometimes failed him unexpectedly, Clara and Caddie sang soprano, and Hetty and Minnie sang whatever came into their heads up or down the scale; but somehow it all came out in a sweet melodious harmony of voices.

"Really, Mother," Caddie said, when they had just triumphantly finished "Annie Laurie," "we ought to travel around and give concerts like the Rainer or the Hutchinson families. I'm sure we're just as good as they are. The celebrated Woodlawns, the Singing

Woodlawns. . . . Wouldn't it be fun to see our names on a concert bill?"

"I'd collect the money at the door," shouted Warren.

"And Clara should be a second Jenny Lind," said Caddie. "Maybe Mr. Barnum would put us to sing in his museum."

"Along with the tattooed man and the *What Is It?*" said Tom disgustedly.

"No," Mother said, her hands straying softly over the tiny keyboard of the melodeon. "No, it's nicer to have something which belongs to ourselves, I think. It's much nicer to sing for ourselves, and think how very beautifully we do it, than to go out and sing for other people's money and perhaps have them look at us coldly and yawn in the midst of our most elegant harmonies."

"Well, now," Father said, "since we've stopped singing to consider our future on the concert stage, perhaps we had better take time for our apples."

"Yes! Yes!" shouted Hetty and Minnie. "It's time for apples. How many tonight, Father?"

"You must find that out for yourselves," said Father.

In spite of the fact that the orchard Father

had planted was doing well for a young orchard in a new country, there were never enough apples to suit the hungry Woodlawn children. During the late summer when Mother dried apples for her winter cooking, the children were always on hand to help with the paring and to speak for the long curls of peeling and the cores. Each child received his or her core, carefully gnawed off all of the good part, and then counted up the seeds. The lucky one who had the most seeds at the end of the day was entitled to a whole apple of his own. There were other things to do with the apple seeds and peelings, too. The girls used them to tell their fortunes.

Rich man, poor man, beggar man, thief,
Doctor, lawyer, merchant, chief.

You said the rhyme over and over until you reached the last seed; and if it came out *beggar man,* then a beggar man would be your husband. If it came out *chief,* as Caddie was always hoping it would, then you would marry an Indian and go away with the tribe to the distant lakes and forests. When you had divined what sort of husband you would get, you could count apple seeds to see what you would ride in, whether it would be

Coach, carriage, wheelbarrow, cart,

and where you would live, whether in

Big house, little house, pigpen, barn,

and whether you would wear

Silks, satins, calico, rags.

Then, to climax all, you could take the long curving strip of apple peeling, swing it very carefully three times around your head, and drop it over your left shoulder to see what initial it would form as it fell on the floor, for that initial would be the first letter of your future husband's name.

Tom and Warren scoffed loudly at all of this, but sometimes the girls half believed it. Anyway it was fun to try. Caddie and Hetty and Minnie had had all sorts of initials in the apple peelings, but Clara always had the same one—a plain, clear C. Tom said that was because a C was the easiest letter an apple peeling could fall into. Clara blushed and said it stood for her own name and meant that she would be an old maid, but Caddie and Hetty said it was because Charles Carey liked Clara and would like to take her sleigh riding if

Clara would ever look at him or smile at him a little bit. Whenever they said that, Clara blushed even more pinkly and stamped her foot and told them to stop talking nonsense. It was great fun to tease Clara and see her blush and stamp her foot.

This winter the Woodlawns had had a gift of a barrel of apples, brought up from St. Louis on the little steamer with the compliments of Uncle Edmund. If the children had been allowed to have their way, the barrel of apples would have been gone in less than a week, but Father believed in making a good thing last. So the barrel of apples was kept in the cellar and on Saturday nights Father would go down with a peck measure, which he would fill full of apples. A peck measure held an apple apiece for each member of the family, and two or three left over.

When Father came to the door with his peck of apples everybody would be ready to scramble. He would roll them across the floor, and the nimblest scramblers got the extra apples. Everybody was sure of one apple, and the fun came in seeing who could pick up an extra one and what he would do with it if he got it. If Clara got one of the extra apples she was likely to cut it up and divide it among the others; if Caddie got it she liked to carry it around with her most of the week, polishing it until it shone and encouraging everybody to run errands for her in the hopes of sharing it. Tom's extra apple was likely to disappear into his pocket and come out unexpectedly on Katie Hyman's desk someday at school. Warren's and Hetty's and little Minnie's prize apples usually went directly down their own "red lanes" with no thought for the future.

Tonight Father had just rolled the peck of apples, and the erstwhile singers had just come up, red and disheveled, with their prizes, when Nero began to bark and everybody heard the sound of sleigh bells in the southwest cutoff.

The younger children ran to the window, gazing through the frosty windowpane across the moonlit fields of snow.

"Why, look! It's a sleighing party!" Caddie cried. "They're talking the cutoff road. They aren't coming by the house at all!"

"It's Charley Carey," Tom cried. "I'd know those fast black mares of his anywhere. It looks as if he's got half the young folks from Dunnville with him."

Clara began to turn the pages of the songbook on the melodeon.

"Let's sing again," she said.

But Mother did not begin to play.

"A sleigh-ride party!" she said. "And Charles Carey's blacks! Clara, you ought to be out there with those young folks. You really ought. Why didn't they come and ask you? It's just the night for a sleighing party."

Clara kept turning the leaves of the song-book as if she had not heard a word. Her apple lay forgotten on top of the melodeon. The sound of the sleigh bells still shivered and sang in the frosty air outside the window, and Nero still barked and ran from door to window begging to be let out.

"Let's let him go," said Tom. "They've no business coming across our place at night. Let Nero run them off."

"Steady, Tom," Father said. "They're friends and neighbors. Let them use the road."

"If they are friends and neighbors," said Mother tartly, "why don't they ask *my* daughter on their parties, too? Clara's old enough to go. They'll use our road, but they won't invite our daughter."

"Oh, Mother," cried Clara, "I wouldn't go—I wouldn't go if it was the last sleigh left on earth!"

"I know why they don't ask her," said Caddie. "Charles Carey is always mooning around waiting to talk to Clara, and she won't look at him at all. She'll hardly speak to him. I don't blame him for getting up a party and leaving her out."

"I think she really likes Charles, too," piped Hetty. "I don't know why she acts so ornery to him."

"If I liked a boy," said Caddie, "the way Clara does Charles, and he had a nice bobsleigh and a couple of spanking blacks, I wouldn't act the way Clara does. I'd say, 'Hello, Charles. When are you going to take me riding in your sleigh?' I'd say."

"Oh, you would, would you?" said Tom between large bites of apple. "And what if he'd say he didn't want you, Miss Forward Face?"

"Well, then," said Caddie, "I'd know how he felt about me anyway, and I could go ahead and put tacks in his chair or sand in his hair or whatever I wanted to do to get even with him. The trouble with Clara is she's too shy."

Suddenly and most unaccountably Clara burst into tears.

"Oh, oh, oh!" she sobbed. "What have I ever done to deserve such a family? Why can't you leave me alone?"

And she ran out of the room and slammed the door behind her so hard that her apple was jarred off the melodeon and rolled unheeded across the floor.

"My goodness! Whatever is the matter with

Clara?" said Caddie in surprise. "We were just talking things over in the simplest kind of way. Now the whole evening's spoiled."

It was indeed. The sound of sleigh bells had suddenly spoiled everything.

Mother started to go up to Clara, but Father laid his hand gently on her arm.

"Leave the girl alone a little while, Harriet," he said. "We've been too much for her this evening. We've been too free with our tongues."

"We didn't say anything but what was true," said Tom. "She behaves the queerest way to Charley Carey. It's her own fault if she doesn't get asked. I expect he drove across our place on purpose to let her hear he could have some fun without her—that's what I think."

"We should have set Nero on them," said Caddie.

"It's too bad," piped Hetty, "if Clara and Charles have got to quarrel, because the apple peelings say that Clara's going to marry Charles. If they're going to fight like cats and dogs it's just too bad."

"What do you mean about the apple peelings?" asked Father gravely.

"It's that silly nonsense the girls play, about throwing apple peelings over the shoulder and seeing what initials drop," said Warren.

"It's more fun to tease Clara because it makes her blush. You couldn't make Caddie blush if you soaked her head in red paint, so it's no fun teasing her."

Father looked at them seriously, his brow puckered.

"You mean to say that you've been plaguing Clara about Charley Carey just to see her blush?"

"Well, it was only for fun," Caddie said.

"I'm surprised at you," said Father. "Clara's hide is not as thick as the rest of yours. Can't you see what you've been doing to her?"

"But if she really likes him," Caddie said, "why should she pretend not to? I wouldn't be so silly as that."

"Let's see," said Mother, "how old are you, Miss Caddie? Thirteen, is it? And Clara is seventeen. She's almost a young lady. Perhaps you'll understand a little better when *you're* seventeen, Caddie."

Caddie still couldn't understand why. It seemed to her that advancing age should bring wisdom with it, and not reduce a sensible girl to such an extremity of tears and blushes as Clara had reached. But nevertheless she saw that somehow they had wronged poor Clara by teasing her about Charles; and she climbed the stairs to bed, feeling not only that a pleasant evening had been spoiled but that somehow she and the younger children were responsible for it.

"They'll be back before long," she heard Father say as he fastened the door for the night. "We'd better leave Nero indoors to-night. He might do them harm if he were out of doors when they came through the cutoff."

Tom and Caddie rubbed shoulders in the narrow stairway as they went up to their rooms.

"We better make it up to Clara some way maybe," said Tom sheepishly.

"Ya," Caddie agreed, but she could not for the moment think how.

Caddie had been asleep for some time when the sound of sleigh bells aroused her. The sleighing party had been out a long time, but now they were returning by way of the short cut. Caddie put her feet over the side of the bed onto the cold floor. The little window of the room which she shared with Hetty and Minnie overlooked the southwest pasture. Hetty and Minnie were sleeping peacefully, but Caddie could hear Nero beginning to growl in the kitchen below. She went to the window and rubbed a clear place on the frosty pane so that she could look out.

The sound of the sleigh bells, so gay and carefree in the middle of the night, made her angry. The sound of young people singing and shouting made her angry. If Clara heard it in her room at the other side of the hall, she was probably sobbing helplessly into her pillow.

"Oh, *seventeen!* Pooh! Pooh!" said Caddie angrily. She pulled on her moccasins and snatched a blanket from her bed to wrap around her shoulders. "I'll fix them," Caddie said.

On the way down the narrow stairway Caddie's shoulder rubbed against something warm and moving.

"Tom!" she gasped.

"Well, what are you doing here yourself?" demanded Tom.

"The same thing you are."

"All right then. Keep still and do it."

They went on down to the kitchen, where Nero was leaping and barking and scratching at the door. Caddie drew back the bolt, and Tom lifted the latch. With a yelp of delight Nero was off across the snow in pursuit of the trespassers.

"I hope Father isn't mad," said Caddie doubtfully.

"I don't care. I hope Nero bites them," Tom said. "Showing off like that to make Clara cry!"

Caddie crept back upstairs and looked out

of the small clear patch on her window. The moon was still bright, and she could see that the sleighing party had stopped to take down the bars of the gate. The sound of the bells had ceased, and the sound of the singing and shouting had ceased also. Nero was still barking, but Caddie could not quite make out what was happening. It looked as if Nero were sitting in the middle of something large and dark, and all the merrymakers were standing about him at a safe distance wheedling and coaxing him.

"Good Nero! Please, Nero. Go away now and let us have it," Caddie could almost hear them saying. She rubbed the frost and strained her eyes, but she couldn't for the life of her tell what had happened. . . . Only it looked—it really looked—as if Nero had the situation well in hand.

At last the young people climbed back onto the sleigh, but they did not sing nor shout. Only the sleigh bells rang a trifle mournfully as they drove away—*without* the large dark object upon which Nero was sitting. Nero was still barking but quite sociably now, with his muzzle turned up pleasantly toward the moon.

"Good old Nero," Caddie said as she climbed back, shivering, into bed. "I guess Tom and I did well to leave it to him."

First thing in the morning she scratched another clear place on the windowpane and looked out. Nero was still there, curled up comfortably on the something large and dark. Tom and Caddie raced out before breakfast, across the snowy pasture to look at Nero's prize. Nero greeted them with wagging tail and a general air of pride.

"By golly!" cried Tom. "It's Charley's buffalo robe! They must have thrown it out at him, and Nero wouldn't let them have it back."

Chuckling with delight, Tom and Caddie pointed out the tracks in the snow where the unfortunate party had stood, just out of Nero's reach, imploring him to give them back the buffalo robe. Finally they had had to abandon it and drive away without it.

Nero was delighted to surrender his prize to Caddie and Tom. He pranced along beside them, wagging his tail, as they carried the buffalo robe up to the house.

"Say, Tom," Caddie said just before they reached the house, "I'll bet Charley Carey will come back to get this thing today."

"I figured on that, too," said Tom. "Let's make sure that the coast is clear, and that Clara goes to the door."

It took some careful managing to get Hetty and Minnie out of the back door on their way to the barn just as Charles Carey came up the front driveway and stopped at the front door. They had taken Warren into their confidence, and posted him as lookout on the rail fence at the corner of the road. When he saw the high-stepping blacks drawing Charley's small sleigh, he had signaled to Tom, who was mending harness on the back step, and he in turn had given the signal to Caddie, who got the little sisters out the back door.

At the first sound of the knocker on the front door Mother had begun taking off her apron; but somehow Caddie and baby Joe had managed to upset his milk at that very moment, and Caddie had cried, "Mother, look at the baby! Come here quick!" At the same time, she shoved Clara into the front hall and shut the door after her.

It was nice that today Clara happened to have on her light blue linsey-woolsey dress that went so well with her pink cheeks when she blushed.

Caddie, helping Mother to wipe up baby Joe's milk, could hear that Clara had taken Charley into the parlor. He was staying ever so much longer than it would have taken to get the buffalo robe and go right away again.

"Oh, dear!" thought Caddie to herself. "I hope she's being civil to him."

"How tiresome!" Mrs. Woodlawn was saying aloud. "Someone at the door, and the baby *would* choose that moment to spill his milk! Whoever can it be?"

She repeated her question to Clara after the front door had opened and closed again, and Clara had come back into the kitchen. Clara just stood there a moment, her eyes very bright and shining and her mouth smiling a little shyly.

"Who was it, Clara?" Mother repeated.

"Why, it was Charles Carey," said Clara in a small, clear voice. "He came to get his buffalo robe."

"I hope you apologized for Nero," said Mother. "I hope to goodness you made yourself agreeable."

"I tried to," Clara said.

"He didn't find the robe damaged in any way, did he?" asked Mother.

"I don't—think—so," said Clara.

At that moment Hetty came bursting into the kitchen.

"Mama! I just saw that Carey boy driving his black horses through our place again. Father's going to have to put a *No Traipsing* sign to keep him out."

"He came," explained Clara, smiling to herself again, "to get his buffalo robe."

"He did?" cried Hetty incredulously. "But look! There it is, right in the hall, and Nero's lying on it!"

The boys and Minnie had come in by now, too, and they all looked where Hetty's finger pointed. She was perfectly right, as always. Charles Carey had come for his buffalo robe, and then he had forgotten to take it with him.

Everybody looked at Clara, and she was blushing quite red all up and down her cheeks; but she said in a clear, steady voice, "Its quite all right if he forgot it, because he's coming back this evening—to take me sleigh riding while the moon's still full."

Nobody said a word. They were all thinking to themselves, "Well, whatever happens, we mustn't tease poor Clara any more."

"Come, Nero," Clara said, "I've got a bone I've saved for you."

She fetched Nero's bone and gave it to him on the back porch. When she came back again, they were all still standing there wondering what to say next. It was the first time the Woodlawns had ever found themselves embarrassed to speak freely.

Clara looked around at all of them and drew a long breath.

"Go on and tease me," she said. "I don't care a bit."

They all began to laugh and everything was happy again and as it should be. Only Caddie was thoughtful.

*"Seventeen!"* she said to herself. "My goodness!"

# 10

## Mrs. Nightingale's House

"Dr. Nightingale stopped by," Mrs. Wood-lawn said, "and asked if one of the girls could stay with Mrs. Nightingale tonight. He's been called way over to Eau Galle, and he doesn't think he can be back till morning."

Clara and Caddie looked at Mother in dismay. They both began to speak at once.

"It's the night of the literary society at the schoolhouse," cried Clara.

"I promised Father I'd help him with the clocks tonight," said Caddie.

Then Clara added very quickly, "Of course, you could help Father any other night, Caddie," and Caddie cried, "Literary society! My goodness, that's just school dressed up in party clothes! Who wants to go to school?"

Hetty stood looking at them without saying anything.

"Of course," said Mother coolly, "the hub of the matter is that neither of you wants to go to the Nightingales'."

"I don't blame them," Tom said. "Mrs. Nightingale's proud, and she doesn't like children."

"How do you know she doesn't like children, Tom? Did any of you ever ask her?"

"No, but the Nightingales haven't got any. It's as quiet as a graveyard around there—not a bit like our house. Anyway," he added, "Mrs. Nightingale's got her father to stay with her."

"Tom, he's past ninety. He'd be worse than no one if there was any trouble."

"But trouble, Mother?" protested Caddie. "What kind of trouble would there be?"

"I don't expect there would be any," Mother said sensibly, "but Mrs. Nightingale is a tiny little thing, and she's always lived in town. That's why they hated to move out here, because the doctor's gone so much at night and she's afraid to be alone."

"A doctor oughtn't to live in the country," said Tom, "unless he wants to be a farmer."

"Hark at you!" cried Mother. "Maybe you don't remember the days when we had to do our own doctoring here in Dunnville. Indeed,

I don't wish those days back again! I'm proud and glad to think a doctor's bought the farm next to us, and so should you be!"

They knew that they were wrong and Mother was right, but it did not alter the fact that they felt strange and uneasy with their new neighbors. Dr. Nightingale was well enough, a tall good-looking man with muttonchop whiskers and a kindly dignity. But there was something almost witchlike about his tiny wife, with her nose like a beak and her shiny bird-black eyes. Did she but sing, Nightingale would have been a fitting name.

"If it weren't that Charley is coming for me—" Clara began. "I don't know how I could get word to him at this late date."

"Why couldn't a boy go as well as a girl?" asked Caddie. "Tom would be more protection than any of us."

"Golly!" cried Tom, with a sudden enthusiasm for the woodpile in the back yard. "I never split that wood Father told me to!"

As he disappeared out the back door, Hetty said suddenly, "I'll go."

The rest of them looked at her in astonishment.

"Well, bless my soul! Why not?" cried Mother. "Such a tempest in a teacup as you've all been raising."

"Oh, Mother," Caddie said, "of course I'll

go. I'm sorry I made a fuss, but Hetty's much too little."

Hetty stood tall.

"I *am not* little," she said in a dignified voice, "and anyway I'm not afraid. I guess that's the main thing, if you go to keep a person company."

"Hetty shall go," said Mother, "and the best of luck to her. It's company Mrs. Nightingale wants, and Hetty's the chattiest one of you. Besides, if there's a message to carry—"

This was not the first time Hetty had sped across the fields toward the doctor's house with her mittens flying behind her by their blue strings and her cap all crooked on her red hair. She had gone to tell them the day their cow got into Father's meadow, and she had been the first to let them know when the circuit rider brought the new preacher. But she had never been inside the house, and now as she sped along she had her own misgivings. Maybe, if Mrs. Nightingale really did not like children, she would be angry to see Hetty come instead of Clara or Caddie. She almost wished for a moment that Minnie, who had begged to come with her, had been allowed to do so. But then she saw that that would have been even worse. If Mrs. Nightingale did not like one little girl, she would dislike two little girls twice as much.

Hetty's usually rapid pace gradually slackened. She sat down in a corner of the rail fence which separated Father's place from Dr. Nightingale's to think if she could remember why it was that she had said she would come. Perhaps it was just because the others had squabbled about it, and suddenly she had felt sorry for somebody whom no one else wanted to be with. There had been so many times in the past when she had wanted to be with Tom and Caddie and Warren and they had not wanted to be with her. It was not that way any more. Since the time they had played the tricks on Annabelle and she had told Mother, Caddie and she had been closer friends and she did not often feel left out. Still she knew how to sympathize a little bit with the doctor's strange small wife.

Hetty sat for a few minutes longer in the fence corner. She opened the little bag which Mother had given her for her things and checked over the contents. A clean outing-flannel nightgown, a hairbrush, her own towel and a square of Mother's homemade soap, and some salt in a twist of paper for washing her teeth. Having a bag with her own things in it—it was like traveling to St. Louis to visit Uncle Edmund! She was on a real, grown-up adventure, no matter how badly it should turn out.

She stood up, put her cap straight on her head again, and climbed over the fence. Before she knew it, she was flying along once more with the mittens standing straight out behind her like very small blue wings.

Mrs. Nightingale came to the door in answer to her knock.

"Was there something you wanted, little girl?"

It was not a very good beginning.

"Maybe you don't remember me," said Hetty, suddenly thinking to put on her mittens just when she might have been taking them off, "but I am one of the Woodlawn girls."

"Oh," said the doctor's wife, "then you've come to stay the night. And which one are you?"

"I am Henrietta," said Hetty, standing as tall as she could.

It helped to make her feel grown-up, to call herself Henrietta, and really she was as tall as Mrs. Nightingale when she held herself very straight.

"Well, come in, Henrietta."

"Maybe you think I might not be very good if Indians came or the house caught on fire or something," apologized Hetty, "but Mother thought I'd do."

"You'll do very nicely," said Mrs. Nightingale. "I'm not really afraid, you see; only, after Papa goes to sleep and when the doctor's away, sometimes the house gets very, very quiet."

"I see," said Hetty.

She and Mrs. Nightingale looked at each other. It was very strange to look directly into a grown person's eyes without having to tip one's head and look up. Suddenly she felt as if she really had traveled—not just across two fields, but into a different sort of place altogether.

"Lay off your wraps," said Mrs. Nightingale, "and then we'll go and see Papa. Supper's nearly ready."

A very sweet, little, round old man sat by the stove in the dining room. He had on large green carpet slippers, and all around his face and in front of his ears he had a fringe of white hair like a frame.

"This is the little girl we were expecting, Papa," said Mrs. Nightingale in quite a loud voice, for it seemed that the old gentleman was deaf.

"Well, well! Indeed?" said the old gentleman. "And what is the little girl's name?"

"It's Henrietta, Papa."

"How do you do, Henrietta? I'm glad to see you."

"Sometimes they call me Hetty."

Hetty's voice was quite loud and clear so that he could understand her. She was beginning to feel at home.

"Yes, yes, indeed," said the old gentleman, smiling as if he were far away in his thoughts or knew some kind of secret which the others did not share.

His eyes were so kind that Hetty knew at once that she would like him and yet, like everything else connected with Mrs. Nightingale, he was somehow surprising.

"What should I call him?" Hetty asked Mrs. Nightingale.

"Just Grandpa, I think," said Mrs. Nightingale.

There was a bustle now of getting the last things onto the table, and it seemed very odd to Hetty to sit down to table with only two other people when there were always so many around the long dining table at home. When they were seated at the table, Grandpa and Mrs. Nightingale folded their hands and bowed their heads, and Mrs. Nightingale nodded to Hetty to do likewise. It was as when Mr. Tanner came; only, instead of making a long, earnest blessing, Grandpa sang a very short one in a high quavering voice. Then he opened his eyes and smiled at Hetty as if he were a little surprised to see her there.

He took up a knife and a fork in a business-like manner and said very pleasantly, "And now, Amanda, will you have sliced ham or a little cold chicken or both?"

Hetty looked around to see where Amanda was, but Mrs. Nightingale nudged her and said, "He means you, my dear."

"Oh, both, please," said Hetty very loudly and hastily.

The plates they ate from were all different. Hetty's was pink with three kittens in a basket painted on the center. It seemed a pity to cover them with ham and chicken and potato hash. Mrs. Nightingale's plate showed a scene from Queen Victoria's coronation, and Grandpa ate off a ferocious-looking American eagle with the Stars and Stripes clutched in one claw and a bundle of arrows in the other.

The bread was in a wicker basket, and there were three kinds of jam and jelly in little dishes shaped like various kinds of fruit. There was honey, too, and it came in a pot shaped like a bee hive with flowers painted against the sides of it and a china bee poised on the cover by way of handle. At home there was only one kind of meat or one kind of jam at a time. Hetty sampled everything, and it all tasted just as good as it looked. Hetty had tea,

too, which she never had at home. It came in
a cup with violets on it, and it was mostly
cream and sugar.

"And where are you going next, Louella?"
Grandpa asked kindly.

"It's Henrietta, not Louella, Papa," said
Mrs. Nightingale in a loud but at the same
time gentle voice. "Don't you remember?
She's come to stay with us tonight."

"Bless my soul! Of course!" said Grandpa,
laughing. "Henrietta, of course!"

After supper, which Mrs. Nightingale
called "tea," Hetty helped her hostess with
the dishes. The kitchen was hardly like a kitchen at all. There were wonderful colored
calendars and almanacs all over the walls.
Mother would have thought one calendar
enough, but Mrs. Nightingale seemed to put
them up for art's sake and not to keep track of
the day or month. There was only one of
which Mrs. Nightingale had not quite ap-
proved. It was a picture of a lady in a low-
necked gown, and Mrs. Nightingale had cut
out a large bunch of red roses from the illustrated seed catalogue and pasted them over
the lady's bare neck.

Everything was as neat and clean as a pin,
and the tea towels were embroidered with
cabbages and turnips.

When the dishes were done up they joined Grandpa, who was sitting by the dining-room stove knitting purple wool into afghan squares. Hetty had never seen a gentleman knit—even such a very old gentleman as Grandpa. She stood and watched him with her mouth a little bit open. Mrs. Nightingale explained it to her.

"He doesn't see very well to read, but he likes to have something to do with his hands."

"Come in, Mildred, and have a chair," said Grandpa hospitably.

Mrs. Nightingale looked at Hetty and smiled just a tiny bit, and Hetty smiled back. It was nice and friendly now that everybody understood about Grandpa's bad memory for names, and Mrs. Nightingale did not try any more to tell him that the little girl's name was Henrietta.

"I'm going to show her the cabinet, Papa."

"The cabinet! Oh, yes! Yes! By all means!"

"Come, Henrietta. The cabinet's in the parlor."

They lighted an extra lamp and went into the front parlor. It was chilly in there without a fire, and Mrs. Nightingale gave Hetty a Paisley shawl to wrap around her so that she should not catch cold.

Hetty had never seen such a wonderful parlor. It was crowded with all sorts of extraordinary things, and on a small sofa beneath the window sat a very large and marvelous doll with a china head and china hair done in the most elaborate fashion and real earrings in her ears.

But, as if all of this were not in the least strange, Mrs. Nightingale led Hetty directly over to the cabinet.

It was a wonderful glass and mahogany cabinet, and in it were many things. Mrs. Nightingale opened the cabinet door reverently and Hetty sank to her knees beside it, her eyes wide with delight.

"Papa collected most of these things when he was younger. I knew you'd like to see them."

"Oh, yes!" said Hetty.

There were birds' eggs and peacock feathers, picture frames made of shells and necklaces made of seeds, pieces of petrified wood and glass globes which contained snowstorms when turned upside down. Mrs. Nightingale took things out one at a time and allowed Hetty to handle them. There was a tiny full-rigged ship in a bottle, and the great white egg of an ostrich. There was a jumping frog made out of one of the vertebrae of a turkey, a rubber band, and a bit of tailor's wax. You held it on the palm of your hand a moment until the wax grew warm, releasing the rubber band, and then the "frog" jumped. There was a little china ballet dancer with a china skirt which looked exactly like lace, and a pair of china dogs with round calico spots and golden collars.

There were many other things, but finally Mrs. Nightingale came to the climax of the exhibit. She took out a large magnifying glass and a very tiny box, and bade Hetty look into the box through the glass. Hetty obeyed and saw two minute figures dressed in foreign costume.

"Fleas, dear," said Mrs. Nightingale. "Yes, really. They are fleas dressed up. Would you ever imagine such a thing? But now I'm going to show you something even more astonishing. Keep holding the glass, and take this pin in your fingers. Don't prick yourself—it's just a common pin—but now read what it says on the head of it."

Suddenly the head of the pin grew large under the magnifying glass, and there was written on it.

Our Father which art in Heaven . . .

The whole Lord's Prayer was engraved on the head of a pin! Hetty read it all through carefully and not a syllable or a letter had been omitted.

"Well, I never!" she said, looking at Mrs. Nightingale in the greatest astonishment.

Mrs. Nightingale looked back at her and smiled.

"It's a wonderful world we live in, isn't it?"

"It certainly is!"

"Well, that's the end of it," said Mrs. Nightingale, putting everything very carefully in its place and closing the glass door.

"Oh, my!" said Hetty, with a long sigh. And then she couldn't help looking around at the doll on the little sofa, and she couldn't help asking, "Who's doll is that?"

"She's mine," said Mrs. Nightingale, laughing a little as if she knew that she was really too old now for dolls. "Her name is Adelaide. Would you like to sit and hold her for a minute?"

"Yes, I would," said Hetty.

Hetty sat on the slippery horsehair chair, and Mrs. Nightingale put Adelaide into Hetty's lap. She was almost as heavy as a baby and she had tiny high-heeled boots and she was dressed in a lovely silk gown of the latest fashion. Hetty touched the dress, the tucked and lace-trimmed petticoats, the boots, the earrings which had real sets in them, with reverent fingers.

"Oh, my!" was all that the chatterbox of the Woodlawn family could find to say.

"She's almost as old as I am," said Mrs. Nightingale. "You see, my birthday comes on Christmas day—which has its disadvantages, as you may imagine. But I was the youngest and the littlest one of the family, and Papa always remembered to give me both a Christmas gift and a birthday present. The Christmas I was ten, when I came down to breakfast, Adelaide sat beside my chair upon her little sofa. The sofa was the Christmas gift, and Adelaide was my birthday present."

"My goodness!" said Hetty.

"I always thought," said Mrs. Nightingale, and suddenly there was an odd sound in her voice, almost like tears. "I always thought I'd keep her until I had a little girl of my own. But the good Lord has never blessed me . . ."

Mrs. Nightingale arose then and lifted Adelaide, gently setting her back upon the small sofa. Hetty stood up, too, and smoothed her dress, and followed Mrs. Nightingale out of the parlor. But when they came to the door, they both stopped and looked back.

"Good night, Adelaide," Hetty said.

The way Mrs. Nightingale was holding the lamp, it made her shadow loom up large against the wall—as tall as an ordinary woman.

Grandpa had left his knitting and gone away to bed.

"He thought my name was Mildred," Hetty said, remembering with a chuckle.

"One of his girls was named Mildred."

"My! I'd like for little Minnie to see the cabinet and the doll sometime."

"Sometime you may bring her," said Mrs. Nightingale. "But I can't have more than the two of you at a time. I don't mind more than two myself; but Papa's so old, sometimes he gets mixed up if many people come."

"Minnie is real quiet," Hetty said. "Mother says that I'm the chatty one."

Hetty had a bedroom all to herself, and the sheets smelled of lavender. Over her bed was a picture of the Good Shepherd bringing in the lost sheep. When she was all under the covers, Hetty called Mrs. Nightingale; and Mrs. Nightingale came and sat on the edge of the bed.

"You must sleep well, Henrietta," Mrs. Nightingale said. "Sometimes one feels a little wakeful in a strange bed."

"I don't feel strange any more," Hetty said. "I felt a little scared when I first came."

"Did you?" Mrs. Nightingale said. "Why, so did I! I never know about strange children. I always like little folks, but I'm not always sure that they like me."

"*I* like you, Mrs. Nightingale," said Hetty.

"You may call me Aunt Molly, if you want to."

Shyly Hetty put out her hand and touched Aunt Molly's. Aunt Molly gave her hand a quick, hard squeeze.

"Now I'll start the music box," she said briskly, "and when it stops playing I expect you'll be asleep."

On the table near the door was a plain wooden box with a handle on the side. Aunt Molly wound the handle as far as it would go, and the box began very rapidly to play "The Beautiful Blue Danube Waltz." Aunt Molly went out and closed the door, and the box continued to play. As soon as the tune was ended, it began again at the beginning—only the longer it played, the slower the tune went.

"Maybe sometime . . . she'll let me bring Minnie, so Minnie can see Adelaide."

*Tum-tum-te-dum-dum*, said the music box, going more and more slowly.

"I think we'll all call her Aunt Molly,"

Hetty said to herself. "But I'll be the first. She'll really be *my* Aunt Molly."

The music box went more and more slowly and finally it stopped. Hetty had stopped, too. She was sound asleep.

# 11

# The Christmas Costume

In the beginning Hetty had planned to take a different one of the children with her every time she went to call on Aunt Molly Nightingale. There must be only two at a time, Aunt Molly had said, because Grandpa was so old and many people in the house confused him.

Every Saturday afternoon that fall of 1865 Hetty went to see Aunt Molly, yet in spite of her early resolution, she always took the same person with her—and it was little Minnie. This was not because the other children did not want to go. Now that they had heard about the cabinet and Adelaide and Grandpa and the music box, they were all wild to go and see for themselves. But Mother would not let them plague Hetty.

"No," Mother said reasonably, "Hetty went when none of the rest of you would go. This is her affair."

The reason that Hetty took Minnie with her instead of Caddie or Clara or Tom or Warren had something to do with her own feeling of importance. At Aunt Molly's she was a tall, big girl named Henrietta. It was a new feeling for Hetty and one that she enjoyed. She could take little Minnie with her and still have that sense of being a superior person in a magical world. But if she had taken one of the older children, her instinct told her that even in Mrs. Nightingale's enchanted parlor she would, like Cinderella after the last stroke of midnight, have become once more plain Hetty Woodlawn.

Mother usually found something nice for her to carry to Aunt Molly's: some fresh doughnuts under a clean fringed napkin or a warm loaf of bread.

"I don't want you and Minnie to be the least bit of trouble to Mrs. Nightingale," Mother would always warn. "You must clean your feet well before you go in on her immaculate floors, and remember to be polite and not too chatty. I'm not at all sure that she likes to have you."

But Hetty was sure. It couldn't have been

pretending that made Aunt Molly's eyes light up when she saw them standing in the doorway.

"Well, I declare! It's Henrietta and little Minnie! Come in, my dears, come in!"

When they had gone in by the dining-room stove to take off their wraps, Grandpa would look up from his knitting, or the nets which he made out of fishline, and smile at them and say, "Well, well! What little gels are these, Molly?"

"You remember, Papa—they're the Woodlawn girls, Henrietta and Minnie."

After they had taken off their wraps Hetty, with little Minnie holding fast to her hand, always went to the parlor door and opened it just a crack to look in.

"Good afternoon, Adelaide," Hetty said softly to the doll on the small sofa under the window, and little Minnie echoed, "Afternoon, Adelaide."

Adelaide never replied but it was not a haughty silence; it was only the amiable silence of a princess who is under an enchantment which prevents her from using her tongue.

After they had paid their respects to Adelaide, they went back to Aunt Molly and asked her if there was anything they could do to help her. Sometimes she had errands for them to run; sometimes she let them help her cut calico squares for her patchwork, or she let them tidy her button box or hold a skein of yarn while she wound it into balls. Once they cut cookies for her with a cutter shaped like a man. When the cookies were placed in the pan, Aunt Molly gave them some currants to put on each man for eyes and buttons. Minnie laughed when the currant eyes went on crooked, and Hetty was obliged to help her put them straight. The currants sat on top of the white dough like black dots; but, after the men had been in the oven for a while, the dough puffed up all around the currants and became brown, and then they were real men with eyes and buttons.

Sometimes the two girls put on their wraps again and went with Grandpa to feed the chickens and gather the eggs. Grandpa could not climb into the loft where the hens were fond of stealing away to hide their eggs, but Hetty's sharp eyes could always find the stolen nests. And the day when Grandpa forgot that he had just finished feeding the chickens and started to do it all over again, Hetty and Minnie were there to remind him.

Then, when all the little chores were done, Aunt Molly would open the parlor door wide and let Hetty and Minnie give Adelaide her tea.

The footstool was the right size for a table with a fringed napkin for a tablecloth; and Adelaide had her own little set of dishes, white with a moss-rose pattern. Aunt Molly let the girls set the table and fetch the teapot-ful of milk from the springhouse, and cookies from the crock in the kitchen. When Aunt Molly did not make men she cut her cookies with a doughnut cutter, and the small rounds from the center of the cookies were always baked and kept by themselves for Adelaide's tea parties.

Hetty always tied one of the small fringed napkins around Adelaide's neck, so that no crumb or drop of milk should ever soil the beautiful silk dress.

"Aunt Molly," Hetty asked one day, "if you have had Adelaide since you were a little girl, how does it happen that her dress is in the latest fashion?"

"Why," said Aunt Molly, "that's because I make her a complete new outfit every year. It's just a custom that I started long ago and have always continued. You see, a dress gets quite dusty and untidy after a year's wear. I like a new dress myself once every year."

"So do I," said Hetty, and little Minnie echoed, "So do I."

"She wore a white India muslin when I first received her," related Aunt Molly, "but you may guess that it got rather soiled from a year's handling. So on the next Christmas I made her a red calico out of some pieces left from a frock of mine. I think I have all her costumes in a box in the attic. Should you like to see them?"

There was never a more unnecessary question. Of course Hetty and Minnie wanted to see them! They hung over the box of costumes as if it had contained Cinderella's ball gown or the coronation robes of Queen Victoria.

"You see the old India muslin is yellowed and worn along the seams with handling; for I was only a little girl then, and Adelaide was really played with in those days. Still I was always proud to keep her nice. When the first year rolled around and it was almost Christmastime again, I said to my dear mother, 'Mama, will you make Adelaide a new costume for a Christmas present?'

" 'Indeed no,' said my mother. 'You are a big girl now and have learned all the stitches on your sampler. Now it is time that you put your knowledge to practical use. You shall make Adelaide's Christmas costume yourself.'

"I was a little bit frightened," said Aunt Molly, "but I went ahead and cut it and sewed it all myself."

Out of the box came Aunt Molly's first attempt at dressmaking. It was a turkey red calico with tiny speckles of black, and it was made with a rather plain skirt and very full sleeves in the fashion of thirty years earlier.

"My goodness!" said Hetty. "Did you make it all yourself, Aunt Molly? And you were only about eleven then, I guess."

"Yes, but if you look you'll see that I didn't make it very well. I was in a hurry toward the last, and you see what long irregular stitches I made along the hem."

"It's better than we could do, isn't it, Minnie?"

"Yes, it is," said little Minnie.

"And every Christmas since that time," said Aunt Molly, "I've made Adelaide a costume."

"Every single Christmas?"

"I don't believe I've missed a one."

Then out of the box came Adelaide's costumes, one by one. Each year, as Mrs. Nightingale had grown older, the dresses were more skillfully made, and soon there were hats and cloaks and shawls added. To look over Adelaide's costumes in order was to see a review of the changing fashions for the past thirty years. One could see how the huge sleeves began growing smaller as the skirts grew wider, and how the enormous coal-skuttle bonnets gave place to the small poke bonnets and caps. How pantalets grew shorter and more ruffled, and velvet cloaks came in with tiny muffs and tippets.

The afternoon when Hetty and Minnie first saw Adelaide's costumes was one of the most exciting afternoons of their lives.

"What if you should ever miss a Christmas, Aunt Molly?" asked Hetty. "Would Adelaide feel dreadful?"

"Poor Adelaide!" said Minnie.

"I expect I'd feel even sadder than Adelaide," said Aunt Molly, smiling. "You see, I've made new dresses for her now for so many years it's become a part of Christmas. If I should ever forget it, or if something should happen to keep me from doing it, I expect I'd feel pretty bad."

"My! I guess you would!" said Hetty, and Minnie echoed, "My!"

At home Hetty and Minnie were never done describing the wonders of Aunt Molly's parlor and the magical strangeness of her whole household. For the first time in their lives they had the experience of telling the older children of the family things which the older children did not know. For the first time Hetty and Minnie were listened to with awe and respect.

"What did the petrified wood in the cabinet look like?" Warren wanted to know. "Did it look more like wood or like stone?"

"Was the little ship in the bottle a brig or a bark? Did it have two masts or three?" asked Tom.

"How big was the ostrich egg, Hetty? Bigger than an orange? Big as a puffball?" This from Caddie.

And Clara never tired of hearing them describe the details of Adelaide's many costumes.

"Did Grandpa remember your names today?"

"No, he called us Emily and Miranda."

"Did he feed the chickens twice?"

"No, only once today."

It was a whole new world of experience which the two little girls brought home from Aunt Molly's house.

But one Saturday afternoon at the end of November when they knocked at Aunt Molly's door, they were surprised to see Dr. Nightingale open it. He was so often away, riding around the country to attend to the sick, that Hetty had almost forgotten how he lived here with Aunt Molly and Grandpa—

and how it was really his house as much as Aunt Molly's.

He was very tall and grave, and now there was a little pucker of anxiety between his eyebrows on his forehead.

"Not today, I'm afraid, little girls," he said. "Come back some other day. We have sickness in the house."

"It isn't Aunt Molly, is it?" asked Hetty.

"No, it's the old gentleman," Dr. Nightingale said. "He's very old, and he's come down with a congestion in his lungs. We don't know yet if he'll pull through. Aunt Molly has her hands full nursing him."

"They don't know if he'll pull through," Hetty reported to the family at home, and little Minnie looked very solemn and as if she might burst into tears.

The whole Woodlawn family was concerned. Even those who knew Grandpa only through Hetty's vivid descriptions of him had become fond of the rosy old gentleman who could not remember little girls' names.

Mother threw a shawl about her shoulders and went across the fields to see if there was anything she could do.

A week dragged by and Mrs. Nightingale's father was no better.

"He's just hanging on by a thread," Mother

said, "I don't know how he's kept going for so long. The doctor says he's done all he could and if anyone can pull the old gentleman through it will be Mrs. Nightingale. She's with him night and day. She can't think of anything else."

Everyone was sad but for Hetty and Minnie the sadness was something special. It was first of all a sadness for Grandpa and then for Aunt Molly and last of all for themselves, for they were suddenly shut away from their Saturday world of enchantment.

They thought of Adelaide sitting alone in the cold parlor, and they wondered if she would understand why there were no tea parties, why no one spoke to her.

Then, as the time kept moving on, another thought came to Hetty. The Woodlawns were going ahead with their own exciting plans for Christmas. Tom was making a little wooden cart for baby Joe; Clara was knitting Father a comforter for his neck to keep him warm on the drives to Eau Galle. Whenever you looked at Caddie she hid something under her apron or cried, "Just a minute, please! Don't come in till I tell you."

Hetty said to Minnie, "You remember about Adelaide's Christmas costume?"

"Oh, yes," said little Minnie.

"I wonder if there'll be one this year. I don't think Aunt Molly had started it before Grandpa got sick."

"Poor Adelaide!" said Minnie.

"Poor Aunt Molly, too," said Hetty. "You remember what she said? If ever she'd forget a Christmas, she said, she'd feel sadder than Adelaide."

"I know," said little Minnie.

"Minnie!" Hetty said. "What if we— Oh, Minnie, I wonder if we could!"

"Do you mean that *we* should make a costume?" asked Minnie, her eyes wide with astonishment.

"You know there was some wine-colored alpaca left from Clara's Sunday dress. If she would let us have it!"

"Clara or Caddie would help us, maybe," said Minnie.

"No," said Hetty. She was very decided upon this point. "No. We're the ones who have had all the good times with Adelaide. We must do it ourselves. Remember the red calico dress Aunt Molly made the first time? Some of the stitches were pretty uneven in that. And we would try as hard as we could."

"But how would we know the right size?"

"We must borrow one of the costumes and bring it home with us."

"But how would we get it?"

"We must go with Mother next time she goes."

Clara gave them the wine-colored alpaca without any difficulty, but it was not so easy to persuade Mother to let them accompany her. She put on her shawl that afternoon and wrapped a clean towel about a kettle of soup which was still warm from the fire.

"No, no," Mother said. "You would just be in the way, girls. This is no time for play."

"Mother, we promise," said Hetty. "We won't be any bother—not any. If we could just go for a minute into the parlor where Adelaide sits."

Clara looked at Mother and smiled. Perhaps their wanting the scraps of alpaca had given Clara an idea.

"Honestly, Mother, I'd let them go," she said. "I don't think they'll do any harm."

And so Mother had relented, and they had been able to get one of Adelaide's dresses without anybody else knowing. It had almost seemed as if Adelaide's eyes had questioned them as she sat so sedately on her sofa in the cold parlor with its drawn shades. Perhaps she was wondering why there was no tea today, and why there had been no party for a long time. Was she perhaps beginning to dream of

Christmas? Was she thinking, "Well, it will be different after I get my new costume"?

"It's going to be all right, Adelaide, I think," Hetty whispered, and little Minnie gave Adelaide a kiss.

They did not see Aunt Molly, and Hetty noticed that the many calendars and almanacs in the kitchen still read *November*. Aunt Molly had not remembered to tear off or fold back the November pages.

And now began a very trying time in the lives of Hetty and Minnie. The difficulty of cutting and sewing a costume for the first time was equaled only by the difficulty of keeping a secret. At last it seemed as if they would never be done by Christmas unless they took someone into their confidence; for the first bodice they made was too small when the seams were taken up, and the sleeves turned backwards instead of forwards as sleeves should do. And so one day they told Clara what they were trying to do.

Clara did not seem at all surprised. It was almost as if she had been waiting for them to ask her advice; and now she showed them how much larger one should cut a garment than it would appear to be when it was finished, and how the sleeves would be all right if they were only reversed. Luckily there was enough material.

Usually Clara was not one to tell things, but somehow the news of what Hetty and Minnie were doing got around the family circle. No one plagued or teased them about it. But the day before Christmas, when they were still taking turns at setting in the tiny stitches (which sometimes grew larger for very desperation), and when the end seemed very nearly in sight, Tom and Warren came in from the woods with a doll-sized Christmas tree. It was really a little beauty, of a most perfect shape, and they had risked their necks in the swampland to get it out for Adelaide. And then it seemed that Clara had baked tiny star-shaped cookies with loops of thread baked into them for hanging them upon the tiny branches, and Caddie had been carving and gilding tiny hazelnut baskets and stringing red cranberries.

Suddenly Adelaide's Christmas had become more important to the Woodlawn children than their own.

Hetty and Minnie grew so excited that the last few stitches on the hem were set in with reckless abandon, but even in spite of that the wine-colored alpaca costume was something to delight the eye.

Mother knew about the preparations now, but she was quite reluctant to encourage them.

"I can't—I really can't have you bothering

them," she said, "until we know that Mrs. Nightingale's father is better."

Then, miraculously, about four o'clock in the afternoon Father came in, stamping the fresh snow from his boots in the back entryway, and he said, smiling around at all of them, "Well, I have good news for you."

"What is it, Father? What is it?"

"I just met Dr. Nightingale on the road, and he says that Grandpa's out of danger."

"He's going to get well?"

"He's going to get well! Furthermore," said Father, looking around at Hetty and Minnie with a twinkle in his eye, "it seems that he's been asking for the little girls who used to help him feed the chickens—Emily and Mildred, the doctor says he called them; but Mrs. Nightingale told him those were the little Woodlawn girls and he should let them know that they might come and see Grandpa for a very few minutes if they were nice and quiet."

Caddie and Clara and Tom and Warren all went across the snowy fields with Hetty and Minnie to help them carry the roast fowl Mother had sent and the Christmas tree with all the decorations—and the Christmas costume.

"We'll wait for you out by the barn," Clara said, "so we won't be any bother and so you'll have somebody to walk home with you after dark."

But first the older ones helped the two little girls put the tree in order and light the one candle which they had tied to the topmost branch. Even in her excitement Hetty felt sorry that Caddie and Clara and Tom and Warren were going to be left outside. Her conscience hurt her now because they had never yet seen Adelaide, nor the parlor, nor the cabinet.

Then Aunt Molly was opening the door for them and crying out with surprise at sight of the little Christmas tree.

"No! It's never Christmas surely!"

"Yes, it is!" cried Hetty. "Merry Christmas, Aunt Molly!"

And little Minnie said, "Yes, it is, Aunt Molly!"

Aunt Molly's face had lost the white, troubled look which it had worn for the last month. Her little black eyes sparkled. She was almost beautiful.

"And you have brought us a tree!" she cried.

"The roast fowl is for Grandpa and you and Dr. Nightingale," said Hetty, "but the tree is for Adelaide."

"Adelaide?" said Aunt Molly. Suddenly her

bright face clouded again. "Adelaide! Why, it's Christmas, isn't it? The first Christmas I ever forgot all about Adelaide. How very odd! I never thought I should—"

"Aunt Molly," Hetty said in an excited rush of words, "I hope you won't be angry with us, but we went ahead and did it. It isn't very good, but Minnie and me, we made the Christmas costume."

"You made the Christmas costume?" said Aunt Molly.

There was something strange in her face, and they could not be sure whether she was glad or sorry. She drew them into the kitchen and closed the door. Then she opened the package they held out, and looked very carefully at the wine-colored alpaca costume without saying a word. She turned the hem inside out and looked at the stitches they had made, some that were very small and neat and some that were in a hurry. Hetty stood inside the kitchen holding the little tree with the candle, and Minnie clung to the back of Hetty's cloak, and they were suddenly afraid that maybe they had done the wrong thing.

"It isn't very good," Hetty repeated hesitantly.

"We got in kind of a hurry," Minnie said.

"What do you mean it isn't very good!"

snapped Aunt Molly. "It's ever so much better than *I* did on *my* first one!"

Then Hetty saw that there was a glint of
tears in Aunt Molly's eyes, and she knew that
Aunt Molly had taken so long to speak because she had wanted to cry instead. It was
quite strange. But when Aunt Molly kissed
them, they knew that everything was all right
—because she had never kissed them before
and this was a happy kiss.

The light of the Christmas candle was
bright on Adelaide's china cheeks. It seemed
to make her eyes dance, and the costume fit-
ted perfectly.

"Papa," Aunt Molly said to Grandpa later
when she had taken the girls to see him for a
moment, "Papa, I forgot Adelaide's Christmas
costume, but these little girls did not. They
made her a beautiful one."

Grandpa smiled his little smile as if he
knew a secret.

His voice seemed far away and strange, but
he said, "Molly, take them in to the cabinet.
Let them choose—let Gertrude and Emily
choose whatever they like out of it, for a
Christmas present from me."

"Anything, Papa?" asked Mrs. Nightingale.

"Anything they want," said Grandpa.

So in a moment they found themselves

standing before the cabinet with the magical power to choose gifts for themselves from its wonderful shelves.

Hetty looked at the dressed fleas, at the pin with the Lord's Prayer engraved on the head, at the little china ballet dancer.

Then she thought, "Caddie would take the ostrich egg, Tom would want the boat in the bottle, Warren would want the petrified wood."

Doubtfully she looked at Minnie.

"What do you want, Minnie?"

"I don't know."

"Go on. Decide."

"I don't know," said Minnie again. She looked as if she were going to cry. She never liked to have to make up her mind by herself. "You choose for me, Hetty."

Suddenly Hetty turned around to Aunt Molly, who was watching them from the parlor doorway.

"Aunt Molly—" she said.

"Take your time," said Aunt Molly. "It's Papa's cabinet. He said you could have anything."

"But I like it better here," blurted Hetty, not exactly understanding what she meant herself. "I don't want to take anything away. Oh, Aunt Molly, what I want is for Tom and

Caddie and Clara and Warren to see it—just
like it is."

"Why, that's easy," said Aunt Molly.
"Bring them over tomorrow."

"Aunt Molly, they're outside now. If they
were very quiet—"

"Dear me!" said Aunt Molly. "They're outside? Of course they may come in."

Little Minnie was smiling now, too.

"And they never saw Adelaide either, did
they, Hetty?"

"No," said Hetty.

"Well, Henrietta, go and call them in,
child."

*"Henrietta!"* thought Hetty.

Once the others were all in the house,
grown-up Henrietta Woodlawn would be
gone again and only Hetty would be left. And
yet tonight, on Christmas eve, it was worth
losing that other self to see the older brothers
and sisters drinking in the wonders of the cabinet.

Hetty ran to the kitchen door to call them,
and her heart was thumping hard with happiness.

# 12

## Caddie Gets a Bargain

Caddie sat on the high seat of the wagon beside Father and looked down at the other children grouped around the wagon wheel.

"Be sure and get something nice, Caddie," said Clara. "Something he can use."

"Something he can wear," said Hetty.

"Something he can eat," said Warren, but a chorus of no's drowned this suggestion.

"Something he will like," everybody agreed.

"And be sure to get a bargain, Caddie," called Tom as the wagon started. "Remember, we all chipped in on the dollar."

As they drove out of the farmyard Father looked at Caddie and smiled.

"Quite a responsibility you have, eh, daughter?"

Caddie sighed.

"If it was just my own money to buy a present for baby Joe's second birthday, that would be easy—but when you have to suit everybody! I'm pretty near sorry it was my turn to go."

"No," said Father. "Just do the best you can and don't let it worry you. In that way you'll have a clear conscience and a tranquil heart."

Father's words were reassuring, and Caddie settled herself to enjoy the drive into Durand and the prospect of a half day to herself in a town which was larger than Dunnville or Eau Galle.

A trip to Durand was always a coveted adventure which the children took by turns. Father would be occupied with the business of the mill and, except for the noon meal with him at the hotel, Caddie would have to amuse herself. She felt confident that she could do that.

The big steamer from St. Louis came up the Mississippi and Chippewa rivers as far as Durand, and then one had to take the "little steamer" or lumber keelboat from there up the Red Cedar River to Dunnville unless he wished to drive as she and Father were doing today. The big steamer brought all sorts of things to Durand which never went on as far as Dunnville. There were little high-heeled boots and feather-trimmed bonnets, gold watches with chains and hair bracelets with gold clasps and wax flowers under glass globes; you could even have your tintype taken if you did not mind having to sit still with your head in a vise for so long.

The Woodlawn children had formed the opinion that whatever was worn in Durand must be the height of fashion, and Clara had particularly begged Caddie to keep her eyes open for any changes of fashion which she should see there on the streets or in the hotel. Caddie was never as acutely aware of fashion as Clara or their cousin Annabelle from Boston. The fine leather bridles in the harness shop, trimmed with little bright-colored pictures under rounded glass, were more to her taste than the latest thing in bonnets. But she knew that, being so fortunate as to make this trip with Father, she must not forget the requests of the brothers and sisters who were left behind. So she remembered to look for changes of fashion as well as a birthday gift for baby Joe.

It seemed to Caddie that the ladies of Durand looked very much like those of Dunn-ville. There was only one who impressed her as looking different and more fashionable than the others. This was a lady who sat at dinner in the dining room of the hotel at a table near the one where Caddie and Father settled themselves for refreshment after they had left the horses at the livery stable.

The lady was all in black, a novelty in it-self, for most well-dressed ladies seemed to prefer color, and she wore a very smart little black bonnet with fully a yard of black crepe hanging behind it. It was a fashion with which Caddie was quite unfamiliar, and she was sure that Clara would be interested. The lady was accompanied at dinner by a fashion-able-looking gentleman in a frock coat and sideburns, and other impressive gentlemen came up to her during the meal and bent over the hand which she extended in greeting in a most romantic manner. Caddie was so im-pressed with this glimpse of high society and fashion that she could already see in her mind's eye Mother, Clara, Hetty, and herself all dressed in similar costumes with yards of black crepe floating out behind and gentle-men with sideburns crowding about to kiss their hands.

Father was seated with his back to the delightful lady, and the meal was nearly over before he began to wonder why Caddie was staring.

"You'd better eat your dinner," Father said. "It'll be a long time till supper. If eyes could eat, you'd be well filled. Better set your mouth to work now. What do you find so interesting?"

"It's a lady," Caddie said. "Father, do you know her?"

Mr. Woodlawn half turned and glanced over his shoulder.

"Well, not to speak to," he said, "but it's Mrs. Langdon. She's a rich widow."

"Rich!" Caddie thought as she hastily finished her meal. "Then what she wears is sure to be the height of fashion."

When they had dined, Father went about his business with a parting warning, "Have a good time, and meet me at the livery stable at half past three. Don't keep me waiting."

Clutching her small, homemade purse with its burden of pennies and nickels contributed by the brothers and sisters for baby Joe's present, Caddie began to walk up and down the main street of Durand to feast her eyes on the windows.

There was a rattle with little silver bells on it in the jeweler's window, but Joe was really too big for a rattle now and this one would be sure to cost much more than a dollar. In the window of the dry-goods store there were some little boots, but Caddie did not know the size and they would be expensive, too.

She had thought of a spotted wooden horse with a hemp tail, such as she had seen once in St. Louis, but when she went into the dry-goods store to inquire, the lady behind the counter said, "Land, no! We only have our toys out at Christmastime."

"What else would you have for a baby, ma'am?"

"I could sell you socks or mittens."

"No, Mother knits him those. We wanted something special—something for a dollar."

"Vests?" suggested the lady. "Safety pins? Two yards of embroidery to trim his petticoats?"

Caddie shook her head.

"Maybe I'll be back later," she said.

Up the street she saw several people going into the millinery store. She was beginning to feel discouraged about the birthday present, but at least she could see what was going on in town.

There seemed to be a great many people crowded into the small millinery shop among the caps and bonnets, and a man's voice could be heard crying "What am I bid, ladies and gentlemen? What am I bid on this beautiful leghorn bonnet with the artificial cherries?"

Several ladies' voices cried out, "Fifty cents!" "Six bits!" "A dollar!" "Two and a half!"

It was all very mystifying until Caddie saw the placard in the window which read:

## AUCTION!
OUR ENTIRE STOCK MUST GO AT BARGAIN PRICES
COME ONE, COME ALL
Thursday at 2 o'clock

"At bargain prices," Caddie thought. "That was the last thing Tom said. 'Be sure to get a bargain, Caddie.'"

Of course it was a little difficult to imagine baby Joe with a leghorn bonnet trimmed with artificial cherries, even at a great bargain; for he would probably eat the cherries and have a stomach-ache afterward.

Caddie stood irresolutely outside the shop looking in the window, and then suddenly she saw what she wanted. It was a small child's hat made of straw with a turned-up brim and red ribbon streamers. It would look beautiful on baby Joe. It would be the perfect birthday present—something he could wear, something gay and pretty, something they could not make at home—and Caddie hoped that it would be a bargain.

She stepped timidly into the store, pushing her way through the crowd. She had never been at an auction before in her life, and her heart was beating fast. Everything happened so quickly and noisily at an auction that it was rather terrifying. The auctioneer lifted up a bonnet, crying out its merits at the top of his voice, and ladies bid for it from all sides. There were even some gentlemen bidding on bonnets for their wives or sweethearts. When the hat with the red streamers should be put up for sale, Caddie wondered if she would ever dare lift her voice. She stood wedged in between people with sharp elbows which dug into her ribs, and held fast to her purse and her courage.

There were some hats, of course, which nobody wanted, and the auctioneer would put two together as an extra inducement and almost give them away.

"Do I hear fifteen cents bid? Twenty cents? Half a dollar? Ladies! Ladies! You are letting the bargain of a lifetime slip away!"

Time was slipping away, too. Caddie could see the hands of the eight-day clock on the opposite wall creeping steadily along. It was nearly three o'clock, and Father had warned her to be at the livery stable promptly at three-thirty. Caddie began to fidget and fume. She had spent so much time here now that if she did not get the hat with the red streamers, she would have to go home empty-handed. What would the other children say to that? Tomorrow was Joe's birthday, and they would never forgive her if they did not have a gift for him. Yet, if she went up to the auctioneer and asked him for a particular hat, he would be sure to see how much she wanted it and put a high price on it. Oh, dear! And if the hat came up at all, would she ever dare shout for it?

Caddie was suffering a good deal of mental anguish when suddenly she saw the auctioneer reach into the window for the child's hat and hold it up.

"Here you are, ladies and gentlemen, a child's hat with red streamers, something a bit unusual for the tots at home. What am I bid now? What am I bid?"

There was dead silence, followed by a choking sound which was Caddie trying to find her voice. Something terrible had suddenly happened to it. As in a nightmare, it seemed that she could not make a sound.

"What!" cried the auctioneer. "Does nobody want this jaunty little hat, this pearl of infant adornment? Are the little children of Durand to run around getting sunstroke for the want of proper head clothing? Think! Ladies and gentlemen, think! What am I bid?"

"Twenty cents," someone said.

"Thirty," added someone else in a half-hearted voice.

Caddie pressed her hands together desperately and made several timid sounds like a rabbit in distress.

"Twenty cents! Thirty cents!" shouted the auctioneer in disgust. "Do you think I would let this little jewel go for that? Look here! I'm going to put another hat with it. An extra bargain, ladies and gentlemen! An extra bargain! *Now* what am I offered! *Now!*"

Reaching into a box beside him, the auctioneer drew out another hat and held it aloft. It was a small black bonnet with a yard of black crepe hanging behind it.

Caddie was shocked out of her timidity. Here was a bonnet like Mrs. Langdon's to be knocked down at a bargain with the hat for baby Joe. What luck! What incredible luck!

She flung up both hands and cried out in a strong voice, "I bid a dollar. Oh, I bid a dollar! Please let me have them for a dollar."

Everybody looked around at the young girl who had stood there so long without bidding.

The auctioneer seemed pleased at her offer. He began to laugh.

"Sold!" he cried. "Sold to the young lady in the brown cloak. It's a smart young lady who knows how to buy for the future. Ladies and gentlemen, this smart young lady is looking forward to the days when she will be a mother and a widow."

People were still laughing as Caddie counted out her dollar's worth of nickels and pennies and walked out of the store with her two hats in a bandbox on her arm. But she didn't care at all if they laughed, because she had got a perfectly smashing bargain. And wouldn't the children be pleased to know that their dollar had bought not only a present for baby Joe but a present for Mother as well!

It was only on the long drive home that something the auctioneer had said began to trouble her. What had he meant about "a mother and a widow"? She had been too pleased with her bargain to take his words very seriously.

"Father," she said, "do you know what? I got a present for Mother as well as Joe out of the dollar. Wasn't that pretty good?"

"Fine," said Father, whose mind was still on the business which he had just been transacting.

"Father—"

"Yes?"

"Mother usually wears colored bonnets, doesn't she? But wouldn't a black, a very fashionable one, look nice with her black silk dress?"

"Why not?" said Father. "I should think it would."

"That's what I thought, too," said Caddie, glad to be reassured.

They all stood around Caddie in the dining room as she opened the hatbox. Her face was shining with pleasure and excitement. Father and Mother and Katie Conroy were there, too, to see what Caddie had bought for baby Joe. The baby himself was the only one not there. He had been left in the kitchen with Nero, so that he would not see his present until tomorrow.

"I got a great bargain," Caddie said, "just like you told me to, Tom."

She took off the lid of the box and held up the little straw hat with the red streamers. It really looked very nice. Everybody exclaimed with pleasure.

"How pretty!"

"The very thing!"

"It ought to fit him, too."

"Don't let him see it. We must keep it for tomorrow."

"But that's not all," said Caddie, laying the small straw hat on the chair beside her. "I told you I got a bargain. I got a hat for Mother, too—the very latest fashion."

"Really?" cried Mother, as pleased as one of the girls. "You got a hat for *me*?"

They all crowded closer, and with a triumphant flourish Caddie drew out the little black bonnet with the yard of black crepe behind it and held it out to Mother.

There was a strange silence for an instant and Mother's expressive face went pale.

"A widow's bonnet!" she cried then, with a kind of shriek. "Oh, no, no! Oh, bad luck! Bad luck! I wouldn't touch it for the world."

"Why, Caddie, that's a widow's weeds!" cried Clara.

Mother threw herself into Father's arms.

"Oh, Johnnie, my dear, you're safe and sound, aren't you? You're feeling well, my darling, aren't you?"

"I never felt better," said Father, smiling and patting Mother's shoulder.

"Oh, take it away!" cried Mother. "The horrid, ugly thing! Don't ever let me look at it again."

Caddie stood still in the middle of the room with the bonnet dangling from her fingers. She was filled with bewilderment and distress.

"There was a very stylish lady wearing one," she said, her eyes beginning to fill with tears.

"But it's only ladies who have lost their husbands who wear them, Caddie," explained Clara seriously.

All the pleasure and triumph of Caddie's day in Durand were draining away. What a dreadful mistake she had made after all!

Suddenly Katie Conroy's pleasant Irish voice cut through the general gloom.

"Sure an' I'd admire very greatly to wear it to me cousin Patrick O'Connor's wake the morn's night, so I would."

"There!" cried Father, putting one arm around his wife and drawing Caddie into the circle of the other one. "We've been needing a mourning bonnet in this household for a long time. We lend our scythes and our whetstones to the neighbors; we carry soup to the sick and lend them our sheets and our bedpans. But what can we do for the dead of the community or for those they leave behind them? A few flowers from our garden in season, perhaps. But that's little enough to do for our friends. Now a mourning bonnet with a yard of good crepe to float on the breezes— suppose the neighbors knew we had a thing like that to lend out when the need arose, eh, Harriet?"

Mother began to dry her eyes. She was already seeing the pleasant possibilities of this. There was no one in the neighborhood who took such delight in giving aid to the troubled and the needy as Mrs. Woodlawn.

"You think we could lend it out?" she quavered.

"Why not?" demanded Father.

"Of course!" Mother said, brightening still more. "What a wonderful idea! We could lend it out for funerals. Why, yes, indeed! Of course!"

Katie Conroy was already trying the bonnet on and turning this way and that before the mirror to see the crepe swish around behind her, and endeavoring to compose her genial features into an expression of grief and suffering.

Caddie was a little bewildered by all of this, but gradually her spirits, which had been so dashed by Mother's superstitious horror of a widow's bonnet, began to rise again.

"And you know, Harriet," said Father, "I think Caddie should have charge of it, to lend out, I mean, when the occasion arises."

"Well—" said Caddie. "All of the children helped to pay for it."

"We'll all be a committee to lend it out," said Tom enthusiastically. "May we, Mother?"

"We'll go out hunting for funerals, shall we, Mother?" shouted Warren.

"Of course, of course," said Mother smiling again. "Why, really, it's just the thing this family's been needing, I believe—just so long as *I* don't have to wear it."

"Oh, Mother," Caddie said, "all I thought was how stylish it looked."

"And how about my Cousin Patrick's wake then? I'd be that stylish, sure I'd do the poor spirit extra honor, I would," cried Mrs. Conroy.

"Let Caddie be the one to say first," said Mother.

Caddie drew a long breath.

"I'd be proud if you'd wear it, Katie. Indeed I would," she said.

"But where's baby Joe's hat?" Clara asked.

They had forgotten the baby's hat entirely, but now they all turned around to look for it. It had certainly vanished from the chair where Caddie had put it.

"Oh, look, will you? Just look!" cried Hetty.

There in the kitchen doorway stood the baby, balancing on his uncertain legs and grinning gleefully. On his head was the beautiful new hat, with the red streamers falling down over his nose. In the excitement over the mourning bonnet he had come in and helped himself to the thing which pleased him most.

"See? Baby—hat," he remarked, and no one had the heart to tell him that his birthday wouldn't come until tomorrow.

Yet Caddie could not help thinking that everything had worked out for the best. For baby Joe was happy a day sooner, and the funeral bonnet had begun its many years of valiant service to the neighborhood.

# 13

## Concerning Cousin Lucy, a Candle at Night, and a High Silk Hat

### 1

The trouble all started, of course, when the second-cousin-twice-removed came from Boston to visit the Woodlawns and to take charge of the household while Father and Mother made a short trip to St. Louis. When Annabelle came from Boston it was all right because, although the children could and did play all sorts of tricks on her, after all she was their own age and a good sport into the bargain. But Cousin Lucy was a very old maiden lady with strict ideas about raising children. Since she had never had any children of her own to test her theories on, the best she could do was to visit her relatives and try her hand at improving their children. It seemed in the Woodlawn family that there was always room for improvement.

Cousin Lucy thought, with some justice no doubt, that Caddie was too wild and harum-scarum, that Hetty talked too much, that Warren was too noisy and untidy, that Clara might have been a greater help to her mother, that little Minnie was lazy, and that baby Joe was spoiled.

Somehow or other Cousin Lucy never had a thing against Tom. She said that he reminded her of her great-uncle Eustis who had fought in the Revolutionary War and had shaken the hand of General Washington. While Cousin Lucy was among them, the other children could not help looking upon Tom with a certain amount of disfavor.

"Tom, dear," Cousin Lucy would say, "fetch my workbox for me, do. If I asked one of the others, it would be sure to be spilled and the colored spools mixed."

And Tom, with a hang-dog look which was a mixture of pleasure at being praised and shame at being considered different from the others, would go and fetch it for her.

While he was gone, Cousin Lucy was likely to air her mind to Mother about the girls.

"They are altogether too restless, Harriet, and forward—dear me! Their backs might be straighter, too. When I was a girl I was required to sit for two hours each day perfectly still with a board strapped to my back to keep me quite erect. You should require the same thing of your girls, I believe, Harriet. See how straight my back is now. I shall never be one of these leaning and bending old women, mark my words! I'm seventy-three, and my back is as straight as a ramrod. There's not a thread of gray in my hair, either."

This was quite true. The children looked with a kind of horrified awe at Cousin Lucy's poker-straight back and the untroubled waves of coal-black hair which framed her sallow face. There was something ageless about this strangely black hair which never varied from day to day. Sometimes Mother's smooth dark hair became disarranged or was dressed in another style. But Cousin Lucy's hair never changed in the slightest degree. Each individual hair lay in its appointed place like something carved on a monument and intended for posterity.

It was Tom who first started the rumor that
Cousin Lucy wore a wig. Cousin Lucy had
gone for a little walk down toward the lake
and she had met a garter snake.

"Tom! Tom! Oh, Tom!" she had cried;
and, when Tom had come running, he had
found her standing on top of a stump with
her skirts held up around her, while the small
green serpent went gliding away through the
long grass.

Tom told Caddie later that the strangest
thing of all was Cousin Lucy's hair.

"It was on crooked," Tom said.

"How could it be?" scoffed Caddie.

"Honest, I swear on a stack of Bibles, it
was. Not a hair was out of place, but the
whole lot was turned a little sideways."

Caddie thought this over a good deal, and
her curiosity grew by leaps and bounds. If
Cousin Lucy wore a wig, did she sleep in it at
night or did she take it off? And if she took it
off how did she look? Was she bald or gray or
redheaded underneath, or what? There must
surely be a way to find out. But, on the whole,
Caddie thought it would be better to wait
until Father and Mother were safely on their
way to St. Louis before attempting it.

Meanwhile Mother made all the last arrangements for her unaccustomed absence

from the farm. Katie Conroy was to have full charge of the housekeeping, and Robert Ireton to have charge of the outdoor work, so that Cousin Lucy would have nothing to do but look after the children.

"And don't take them too seriously, Cousin Lucy," Mother warned. "On the whole they are very good children, and I am afraid that you will just worry yourself if you try to keep too high standards of behavior."

Cousin Lucy only tossed her head, because it was really useless for an inexperienced young woman like Mother to try to tell Cousin Lucy anything about children.

After Mother and Father with baby Joe had gone away, Cousin Lucy began to insist upon a whole new set of table manners. The children were required to sit very still with their hands folded in front of them on the tablecloth until food was placed before them. They were not to speak until spoken to. They must say *"S'il vous plaît"*—which was some sort of barbarous foreign language—instead of "Please," and *"Merci"* instead of "Thank you."

"What do we say in that language for 'You're welcome'?" Warren wanted to know.

But Cousin Lucy just tapped her spoon against her glass and said very haughtily,

"How many times have I told you not to speak until you are spoken to, Warren?"

If their milk or tea were hot, Cousin Lucy allowed them to pour it into their saucers, but she insisted that when lifting the saucer to the lips, the little finger should be raised in the air to show good breeding and delicacy.

"See how Tom does it, children!" cried Cousin Lucy. "So like my uncle Eustis—so very, very like!"

Tom blushed and shuffled his feet uncomfortably under the table, but nevertheless he couldn't resist crooking his finger like the finger which had lain in the palm of General Washington.

Cousin Lucy also made changes in their sleeping arrangements. She made a sort of dormatory for the girls out of the large room which Mother and Father and the baby usually occupied. She had Robert Ireton and Tom Hill up from the barn to move around the beds, so that Clara and Minnie, Caddie and Hetty should all sleep in the same room with her.

"To see that they keep out of mischief," said Cousin Lucy. "As to the boys, I shall leave it to Eustis, I mean Tom, to keep his little brother Warren in good order."

Tom coughed apologetically but he

couldn't help feeling important. Usually Clara's judgment was considered before Tom's in family council; but Cousin Lucy looked over Clara's head as if she scarcely existed, and hit upon Tom as the wisest and most reliable of the children. It was difficult not to be flattered.

Of all the girls, only Caddie was pleased about the new sleeping arrangements.

"Cousin Lucy, may I sleep in the very next bed to yours, *s'il vous plaît?*" she asked.

Cousin Lucy looked at Caddie thoughtfully. Was it possible that she had been mistaken in thinking Caddie a tomboy, a forward minx, and not at all a lady? No, she decided, she could not have been mistaken, for at the back of Caddie's eyes there was still that little gleam of mischief which frightened her.

"Yes, of course, my dear child," said Cousin Lucy. "I can look after you so much better if I have you beside me."

"Oh, thank you! I mean, *Oh, mercy!*" said Caddie very politely.

"I don't know why you want to sleep next to her," complained Hetty later. "Goodness knows we have enough of her all day without at night, too. I wish Mother was home."

"Listen, Hetty," said Caddie, "if you were real, real curious about something, wouldn't you try to find out? You know, like Columbus being curious about if the world was round and discovering America—like that, you know."

"Well," admitted Hetty, who did not quite follow this train of thought, "I guess it was a good job to discover America."

"Of course it was," said Caddie, "and you'll let me keep the candle and the sulphur matches on my side of the bed, too, won't you?"

"Well—" said Hetty.

Cousin Lucy insisted that everyone should go to bed early, and she herself came upstairs about an hour after they had retired, undressed herself in the dark so that she would not disturb them, slept very briefly, and was the first one up in the morning.

When she was dressed, in the early hours, she would make the rounds of the girls' beds, tapping their fingers with her comb and exclaiming in a vigorous, morning voice, *"Wherefore now rise up early in the morning,* says the Bible. First Samuel, twenty-nine, ten."

If this did not immediately produce the desired effect, Cousin Lucy was not above sprinkling them with drops of cold water from the wash pitcher to bring them out of bed in a hurry.

Caddie was a sound and peaceful sleeper, and for several days she tried in vain to stay awake until after Cousin Lucy had come upstairs and gone to bed and to sleep. Somewhere along the way Caddie's eyes were sure to close and her mind drift off to dreams. At last she was forced to take Hetty into her confidence to the extent of allowing her to tie their big toes together with a short piece of stout string. Hetty was puzzled, but ready to cooperate.

"You see, Hetty dear, I want something to wake me up in the middle of the night. And if you turn over and pull my toe, it will do that."

"But why do you want to wake up in the night, Caddie?"

"I'll tell you honestly," said Caddie. "I want to see what Cousin Lucy looks like after she has taken off her w——, I mean her clothes."

"Well, I want to see, too, then."

"The string on your toe will probably wake you as soon as it does me. But whatever you see, you mustn't say anything, Hetty. Remember."

"Why, I *never* say anything, Caddie," protested Hetty. "You'd ought to know that!"

It is very uncomfortable to sleep with your big toe tied to another person's big toe. Caddie and Hetty must have been jerked awake half a dozen times before they knew by the gentle and refined snoring in the next bed that Cousin Lucy was in for the night and sound asleep.

Cautiously Caddie sat up in bed, with a warning hand on Hetty's arm to remind her to keep still. Through the window drifted a faint gleam of moonlight, together with a smell of clover. Caddie felt along the bedside table for the candle and the matches, and there they were where she had put them. The scratch of the match sounded loud in the quiet room. There was a spurt of blue light, followed by a smell of sulphur, and then the yellow gleam of the candle threw a little circle of light in the darkness. Caddie and Hetty sat up side by side in bed, Caddie holding the candle aloft and both of them gazing earnestly at Cousin Lucy's bed.

The ladylike snoring had ceased with the scratching of the match. In her bed Cousin Lucy sat up also, dazed and wild-eyed—and yes it was true! She was quite, quite bald on top of her head—as bald as Mr. Adams, the grocer!

Poor Cousin Lucy gave a little scream, but not before Hetty had cried out in astonishment at the top of her voice, "Oh, Cousin

Lucy, you've lost—you've lost—you've *lost* your *hair!*"

Clara and little Minnie sat up, too, gazing in sleepy-eyed wonder at the spectacle of Cousin Lucy hastily trying to put on her wig and crying in a terrible voice, "Put out the candle! Put out the candle! For mercy's sake, put out the candle!"

Caddie blew out the light and sank back on the pillow. There was a long and ominous silence in the dark room which none of the girls dared break before they finally drifted off again to sleep.

The next morning Cousin Lucy did not tap their fingers nor sprinkle water on them to wake them up. They awoke in their own good time and went rather sheepishly down to breakfast. Cousin Lucy sat at table, her back very erect and not a black hair out of place.

She said in a crisp voice, "I allowed you young ladies to sleep this morning because you were very restless during the night. I am convinced that it was something you ate which caused your disorder. You were troubled with the most fantastic nightmares, and at one time I was obliged to cause the candle to be lit to quiet your fears. I trust that by this morning you will have entirely forgotten the subject of your nightmares, and realize that they could only have been caused by a disordered digestion and a too active imagination."

"Yes, Cousin Lucy," they said as meekly and hastily as possible.

"Still and all—" began Hetty, but Caddie nudged her so violently that she broke off and said nothing further.

It began to seem as if they were going to get off without a bit of punishment. Perhaps the girls did actually begin to wonder if it could have been a dream that Cousin Lucy, as bald as the grocer, had sat up in bed crying, "Put out the candle!"

But in the afternoon Tom, who had been to Dunnville on errands for Cousin Lucy and who was entirely ignorant of the girls' adventure of the previous night, came bursting into the house waving his cap and shouting, "Oh, golly! What do you think? There's a real entertainment coming to Dunnville. They've got out hand dodgers, and bills are stuck on all the fences. A magician! Think of that!"

"Dr. Hearty?" cried the children.

"No, not a medicine show—a real one where you have to buy tickets and all. He's a hypnotist, too! It's to be in the schoolhouse tomorrow night. Oh, say, Cousin Lucy, can we all go?"

Cousin Lucy looked at the four girls, and her face went slightly puckered and sour.

"Oh, please, Cousin Lucy!" cried Caddie. "I mean, *s'il vous plaît.*"

Cousin Lucy pursed her lips.

"It does not appear to be the sort of entertainment for refined young ladies," said Cousin Lucy. "Not at all. Eustis, I mean Tom, may go, of course. He's quite fifteen now and a very reliable boy, but the rest of you shall certainly stay at home and retire at the usual hour."

"Oh, Cousin Lucy!"

"You have heard my final word," said Cousin Lucy.

"But Warren," begged Caddie, who understood perhaps better than any of them that there might be justice in keeping herself at home, "surely Warren can go with Tom."

"Warren's just a little boy," said Cousin Lucy, "and I'm responsible for all of you. Tom is the only one I can trust to go out to an entertainment of this kind at night."

"But, if *you* came with us, Cousin Lucy, couldn't every one of us go?" begged Tom. "Father and Mother would let us if they were here, I know."

"I do my duty as I see it," said Cousin Lucy firmly.

2

Tom was sorry for the others at first and very regretful, but as the time approached when he was to be the only one reliable enough to go, it is no wonder if his head began to swell. He had never before escorted a girl to a party or entertainment in his life— except, of course, his sisters. But no boy ever counts his sisters. Cousin Lucy gave Tom some money for his ticket, and Tom had a little money of his own.

The next day, blushing furiously and trying to appear very offhand, Tom went into Dunnville and invited Katie Hyman to go to the performance with him. She shook her curls over her face and couldn't speak at all for several moments; then she ran to ask her mother, who said that she could go. Tom bought two tickets for the evening, and he had never felt so completely grown-up and a man-of-the-world as he felt that afternoon.

As he went home along the dusty road he suddenly wondered what he was going to wear for such a grand occasion. He would wear his best suit, of course; but it was getting a trifle small for him—or rather he was getting large for it—and it would shed no particular glory upon his manly figure. He pondered what he could possibly do to improve it. A flower from the garden in his buttonhole would help, a nice bit of heliotrope or a red geranium. But *what* to wear upon his head? The thought of his old cap which he had used for carrying nuts and marbles and birds' eggs, and even a frog upon one occasion, and which he had so often carelessly tossed about and ill used—the thought of his cap did not please him. There was nothing of Warren's which he could possibly borrow either. That was the only disadvantage of being an elder brother—you could not rely upon hand-me-downs in case of an emergency. As Tom thought his situation over, an incident connected with Mother's and Father's departure presented itself to his mind.

He could remember hearing Mother say to Father, "Johnnie, you must take your high silk hat along. You'll certainly need that in St. Louis."

And Father had replied, "Oh, for pity's sake, Harriet! Don't make me wear that stovepipe hat. 'Twill spoil all the pleasure I'm going to have out of this trip, if you do."

"You never wear it!" Mother had cried. "I don't know why you ever bought it."

Father had laughed his good-natured laugh

and said, "I guess I bought it to hand down to Tom. Wait a few years until he begins to escort the young ladies. I expect he'll make good use of it then."

Tom went up into the attic and opened the bandbox and took out Father's hat to look at it. It was very beautiful and tall and black and shiny. He was glad that Mother had not insisted on Father's taking it. After all, Father himself had said that someday it would belong to Tom. "Wait a few years," Father had said, but Cousin Lucy considered Tom grown-up already, and he was certainly beginning that very night to escort young ladies. Father could hardly have made the slightest objection, Tom thought.

But somehow Tom did not have the heart to put the hat on before he left home; even Cousin Lucy might have objected, and he could not have endured the wistful, even reproachful glances of the girls and Warren.

He smuggled it out of the house in its bandbox and hid it in the corner of the rail fence nearest to town. Fortunately it was a bright clear evening and the dew had not yet started to rise. As he hurried to retrieve the hat on his way to town, Tom had a horrid premonition that a gopher or a woodchuck might have started dining on it. But it had not been harmed in any way. Tom, with all his new-found feeling of importance, was very anxious that no harm should come to the high silk hat. One didn't trifle with Father's possessions even if they might someday be one's own. No, the hat must be returned in perfect condition.

Katie was dressed in one of the pretty dresses which her mother knew so well how to make, and she had a very pretty little homemade bonnet over her curls. At first she would not look at Tom at all, and they walked along on opposite sides of the road as if they had just chanced to be going in the same direction at the same time without having a speaking acquaintance.

Finally Tom mustered up his resolution and said, "It's a pleasant evening, Katie."

Tom had had Father's hat in his hand when he went up to the door for Katie, and since she had not looked at him again, she was unaware of its splendor. Now, as Tom ventured this bold remark, she raised her eyes to say a faint "Think likely," and saw for the first time how magnificent he was. All power of speech and motion left her for a moment, and she could only stand in the road and stare.

At last she found her voice and said, "Oh, Tom!"

Tom understood this as a compliment and so it was intended.

By the time they reached the schoolhouse they were walking on the same side of the road, and Tom was too much filled with his own importance to mind the jeers of the other boys, who were undoubtedly jealous because they did not have high hats on their heads and the prettiest girl in town on their arms.

Tom had started in plenty of time and now they had their pick of the seats.

"Let's sit up front, shall we, Katie?" said Tom. "Because I'd like to see just how the magician does his tricks."

"All right, Tom," said Katie.

They sat on the front bench, and Tom carefully balanced Father's hat on his knees, smoothing it from time to time and flicking imaginary specks of dust off the crown.

The schoolhouse seemed quite strange tonight, and a very magical place, indeed, even before Signor Mephistino began to do his tricks.

The performance started with a demonstration of hypnotism. Signor Mephistino called for volunteers from among the young men in the audience, and Tom was dying to go, but Katie held on to the sleeve of his jacket and looked so frightened that finally he sat still. He was glad afterward because the boys who volunteered only made sport and laughter for the audience. Obediah and Ashur Jones had been among the first to go up, looking tough and resolute, and in a few moments, with some mysterious passes of his hands, Signor Mephistino had reduced Obediah to picking imaginary violets off the schoolroom floor and Ashur to throwing kisses to the ladies. Sam Flusher was made to believe that the teacher's chair was a bucking horse and he rode it all about the platform, "Gee-up!"-ing and "Whoa!"-ing as big as life. The audience nearly went wild with pleasure at these demonstrations.

The second part of the program was devoted to illusions and tricks of magic. There were card tricks which mystified everyone, and out of a simple handkerchief the Signor produced a dozen brightly colored flags. He borrowed a half dollar from one of the deacons and made it appear in George Custis' pocket. Katie screamed when he shot a pistol, and a pigeon materialized from thin air and went fluttering up to sit in the schoolhouse rafters. What an amazing evening!

And then Signor Mephistino looked all over the audience and asked, "Is there a gentleman in the house who will lend me a high hat?"

High hats were not common in Dunnville,

and nobody seemed to have worn one except Tom.

"What? Does nobody have a high hat? I *must* have a high hat!"

Tom felt his heart begin to pound. If something should happen to Father's hat— But Katie had no such qualms. She only knew that Tom had a wonderful new hat which she admired very much, and which was just exactly what the gifted Signor was asking for.

"Tom," she whispered, "look! He wants to borrow your hat. Go on and let him, Tom!"

Before Tom knew what she was doing, Katie was proudly holding it out for everyone to see that Tom Woodlawn was the only boy in town stylish enough to have a high hat, and Signor Mephistino was accepting it from her with a gracious bow.

"Thank you! Thank you!" the Signor said. "We'll endeavor not to do it any harm. Accidents might happen, of course, but we'll hope for the best."

Tom's heart sank to the soles of his boots. He tried to make a protest but his voice stuck in his throat, and Katie was smiling at him so kindly and proudly, as if she had done him the greatest service! With a horrible uncertainty Tom saw the magician's hands making mysterious passes over Father's high silk hat;

he saw it being swished through the air, now top side up, now bottom side up. He saw it being exhibited to the audience to show that it was empty. Then it disappeared for an instant under a red silk handkerchief, and when the handkerchief was removed, Signor Mephistino lifted a live and kicking rabbit out of Father's hat by its ears.

"Oh, Lord," prayed Tom very earnestly within himself, "make the rabbit have nice clean feet."

"And now," cried Signor Mephistino happily, as he put the rabbit into a small wire cage, "now the greatest triumph of all. Ladies and gentlemen, I am going to fry an egg in the young gentleman's silk hat."

Tom half rose in his seat, his mouth making futile noises, but it was too late. With the greatest charm and grace the Signor was already breaking an egg into the crown of Father's hat!

"A real egg, ladies and gentlemen. You are able to observe that, are you not?" and he tossed the two halves of the broken shell into the audience so that everybody, including Tom, could see that it was a real egg.

Next the Signor lighted a match and passed it back and forth under the crown of Father's hat, which he held aloft with the other hand.

It hardly seemed that the one match could have fried the egg; but when the magician held up the hat for everyone to see, there it was in the bottom of the crown—a fried egg!

The rest of the performance passed in a haze before Tom's blurred vision. He was trying to calculate how long it would take him to earn enough money working for Mr. Adams at the store to buy Father a new silk hat. And could he possibly replace it before Father returned? And if not, would Father or Mother be likely to look into the bandbox before the hat was finally replaced?

Then the performance was over, and the magician was passing the hat back to Katie, and Katie was saying in her soft little voice, "Well, Tom, I guess we'd ought to go now." When they were out of the schoolhouse door into the cool blue night, Katie passed him Father's hat and said, "Put it on now, Tom. It looks so nice!"

Tom stopped and took the hat and turned it over slowly for a dreadful moment before he looked inside the crown, and then—oh, wonderful to relate—he saw that it was empty, and clean, and as if nothing had ever happened to it!

"Tom," said Katie when they were almost

to her door. "Do you believe in magic—really, I mean?"

Tom didn't know what to say at first. Ever since the time when he had found that the hired men, instead of the dark powers, had hidden the magical melons under the straw in the hayloft, Tom had resolutely put the possibility of magic out of his life. But the wonder of the fried egg in the silk hat was still strong upon him.

"Well, Katie," he said, drawing a deep breath, "sometimes, I guess, I do. Some of those tricks are mighty hard to explain."

"I'm glad you do, Tom," Katie said. "It's more fun that way than trying to explain everything."

Tom did not wait until morning to put Father's hat carefully away in the corner of the attic where it belonged. He thought now that even if Father gave it to him someday he might decide he didn't care to wear it. Still it had been a lovely evening, and first thing in the morning he meant to set about doing something nice for Warren and each of the girls to make up for Cousin Lucy's keeping them at home.

When Mother was at home again, she said to Clara and Caddie, "You know there was one thing I meant to tell you before I went away. I hope you didn't discover it and plague her about it."

"What, Mother?"

"Well, you know, your Cousin Lucy wears a wig. Poor dear, when she was a girl some plaster fell on her head—and all the hair came out, never to return. But I know if you discovered it you were too well bred to let her see you knew."

Caddie and Clara looked at each other and sighed.

"Mother, I don't know why you think so well of us," said Caddie.

They were a little more patient with Cousin Lucy after that, but never what you might call fond.

When she was leaving to return to Boston, Mother said, "Now, children, Cousin Lucy has been very good to stay here with you. I want you to show proper grief at her departure."

They were so happy to have Father and Mother at home again that they wanted to please Mother in everything—even in the matter of showing grief for Cousin Lucy. So they took the matter into council, and when Cousin Lucy departed she was touched and possibly surprised by the red eyes of the six children and the genuine tears which coursed down their cheeks.

"Maybe I sometimes misjudged them," she thought charitably as she kissed each one good-by.

There was the strangest smell of raw onions about them that day when she kissed them! It almost made Cousin Lucy's eyes water. But she forgave them even the smell of onions because of their tears of grief.

# 14

## Be Jubilant, My Feet!

The Woodlawn girls were all getting new white dresses for the Independence Day celebration at Eau Galle.

"It really seems a waste of good material to make one for Caddie," said Mother, with a sigh. "She's ruined every white dress we ever made for her."

"But she's doing so much better now, Mother," said Clara gently. "Ever since that time when Annabelle was here and she and Tom played all the tricks, Caddie's been trying very hard to be a lady."

"I know," Mother said. "I'm proud of her, too. She's come a long way. It's only that there's something fatal about the combination of Caddie and a white dress. Either she tears it, or she cuts her finger and stains it with blood, or she sits on the grass and gets grass stains, or she accidentally spills a bottle of ink. There's no telling what will happen to this one."

"Well," said Mrs. Hyman, who, with Katie, had come to spend the week at the Woodlawns' while the dresses were being made, "well, you've got plenty of extra material. I'd keep it if I was you, and later on I can always put in a new skirt breadth or a front to the bodice, if she spills or tears."

"That's true," said Mother, "and we'll just have to hope for the best, although all of my past experience tells me that the worst will happen."

Caddie and Katie came in just too late to hear these dire predictions. They had been to the far field to take a bucket of spring water to the men and boys who were haying. Their cheeks were red and their eyes bright. Shy Katie, so timid and fearful at school and at home alone with her mother, blossomed like a rose in the midst of the hearty, happy-go-lucky Woodlawns.

"Come, now, Caddie," said Mother. "You're just in time to have a fit."

The phrase delighted Caddie.

"Run away now, children," she called to Hetty and Minnie, who were trailing along behind her. "I'm going to have a fit."

She slipped out of her old blue denim and into the yards and yards of white muslin, which Mrs. Hyman slid over her head.

"Mind the pins now and the basting threads. Don't pull and squirm too much."

Caddie regarded herself in the mirror.

"Is that me?" she said. "My goodness! I won't know how to act out of blue denim."

"You act like a lady, that's what you do," advised Mother. "You take small steps and turn out your toes when you walk, and keep away from horses and the snags on rail fences, and don't sit on the grass or climb the hay-mow or eat strawberries or write with ink."

"I might as well be dead," said Caddie, screwing up her nose. "Is a white dress worth it?"

"Oh, yes," said Katie. "You look lovely, Caddie. Honest, you do."

"Mother," said Caddie, her eyes twinkling, "they're going to have a log-rolling contest in the millpond at Eau Galle. I can walk logs just as well as the lumberjacks. Will you let me enter?"

"Now, Caddie," cried Mother, vexed beyond measure, "don't let me hear of such a thing! Don't even let a thought like that enter your head. The idea!"

"We'll keep her busy enough singing," said Clara. "The girls are all to sing, in their white dresses with loops of red, white, and blue bunting over one shoulder and knotted at the waist. There won't be time for walking logs."

"Well, see that there isn't!" said Mother tartly.

There never was such a celebration as they had at Eau Galle that year. The lumbering out had begun in the forests along the rivers, and from far-distant camps men came down on log rafts to spend the holiday. The celebration centered about the mill. The loading platform at the back was turned for the day into a speaker's rostrum and hung with flags and bunting, while the open ground beyond was reserved for people to sit with their camp-stools and their picnic baskets. The picnic itself was to take place a little farther up the river in the shady place overlooking the mill-pond, which was to be the scene of various water sports. There was a place for land sports, too, and a poplar tree, stripped of its bark and branches and greased to make climbing difficult, had already been set up with a ham tied to the top as a prize for the first man or boy who should successfully climb it.

Caddie cast a regretful glance at the pole. *Well, that was no place for a white dress, at any rate,* she thought.

Catching the greased pig would not be proper sport for her either, she decided regretfully. Mother never contrived fine clothes for the boys on the Fourth of July because they were expected to get into everything, but the girls were dressed up like china dolls and expected to stay sweet and spotless.

"Oh, well," Caddie told herself, "I *will* be clean and ladylike this year, no matter what. I'll just surprise them all for once."

Father had brought them all over early in the big hay wagon, together with Robert Ireton and Mrs. Conroy, Katie and her mother, and the McCantry family. It had been great fun—all riding together and talking and laughing, and practicing the songs which they were to sing later.

> O hark! O hear! how soft and clear
> The echo's mellow strain!
> O echo, hear! O echo, hear!
> Reply again, again, again—again!

The music floats in softest notes
Upon the zephyr's wing;
O hear the song! O hear the song!
Again we sing, we sing, we sing—we sing!

The sunshine seemed more golden on a day like this, and the smell of new-cut hay and clover bloom far sweeter than it was on ordinary days. Their own singing and the singing of the meadowlarks and red-winged blackbirds along the wayside seemed to mingle in a perfect harmony.

To celebrate the Fourth of July meant something definite in those days. Beyond the picnic lunches, the spread-eagle speeches, the greased pole, the water sports, and the fireworks in the evening, there was the consciousness of happiness and good fortune. It was a day in praise of freedom. The Civil War was still close enough, and even the War of the Revolution, to make them thankful for peace and liberty. It was a kind of summer Thanksgiving Day when they could raise their voices in gratitude for life, liberty, and the pursuit of happiness, and dedicate themselves anew to self-evident truth that all men are created equal.

Father's voice, full of the fervor of the day, started them all to singing "The Battle Hymn of the Republic," and Caddie's heart swelled as she sang. Best of all she loved the fourth stanza.

> He has sounded forth the trumpet
>     That shall never call retreat;
> He is sifting out the hearts of men
>     Before His judgment seat;
> Oh, be swift, my soul, to answer Him!
>     Be jubilant, my feet!
> Our God is marching on.

She kept humming it to herself as she and Emma and Katie wandered about the picnic grounds at Eau Galle.

> Oh, be swift, my soul, to answer Him!
>     Be jubilant, my feet!

Today her feet, in neat white slippers with satin rosettes, were jubilant indeed. The sky was very blue, and the hot sweet smell of new-cut lumber filled the air with a perfume as pleasant as the smell of clover.

The three were early enough to greet the other girls as they arrived in their white dresses with red, white, and blue bunting looped over the shoulder and knotted at the waist. Maggie, Jane, Lida—all of them arrived in due time, with their hair unnaturally frizzed out, from an uncomfortable night in curl papers, and their eyes sparkling with anticipation. All the girls of Dunnville and Eau Galle were to sit on the loading platform behind the speakers, and sing before and after the speeches were delivered. But until the speaking began they were free to roam about as they wished.

Tom and Warren with a crowd of boys went past them toward the millpond, and Tom called back over his shoulder, "They're starting to roll logs. You better come watch."

"Let's do," said Caddie to Katie, and Katie said, "All right."

"Just look out for your dress, that's all," warned Clara. "Mother will be wild if she sees you standing up to sing and the front of your dress all torn."

"Oh, bother!" Caddie said. "They're always plaguing me about my clothes. But nothing— *nothing's* going to happen to this one!"

A good many children were crowded along the banks of the quiet millpond watching the preliminary log-rolling contests. Caddie saw Hetty and Minnie and Pearly and Ezra McCantry playing "I Spy" with some of the other little children higher up the bank.

In the millpond floated several large peeled

logs, and men from the various logging camps up the river were trying their skill upon them. From a boat each man would carefully mount his log and balance himself on it while he rolled it under his feet. He appeared to be running on top of the water, and it was exciting to see how long he could keep it up. Much skill was required to stay on the slippery logs at all, and sooner or later one of the men would lose his balance, slip off, and go down with a great splash—to emerge again almost immediately, grinning and ready to try once more. Walking logs in the river was part of the lumberjacks' job, and they were surprisingly expert at the difficult feat of staying on top while the log rolled under them.

The children soon had their favorites among the contestants, and cheered or shouted praise or disapproval. When Robert Ireton came out in old blue jeans with his strong brown arms folded across his bare chest, waiting for someone to row him to a log, the Woodlawn children and all the children of their neighborhood went mad with glee.

"Robert! Robert!" they shouted. "We're on your side, Robert! Beat the lumber camps, Robert! Show 'em Dunnville's got the champion log roller of the world!"

None of them had known that Robert was going to enter the contest, and Caddie went as wild as the boys, shouting, "Robert! Robert! Lick the old tar out of 'em, Robert!"

The little children left their game of "I Spy" and came crowding down to the water's edge between the legs of taller people, echoing, "Robert! Robert! Beat 'em, Robert!"

Near the shore floated a number of smaller, unpeeled logs, left no doubt from one of the large log rafts which were floated down the river to the mill for sawing. Hetty and Minnie and the two little McCantrys came to stand in front of Caddie and Katie, and Caddie saw Ezra's toe go out experimentally to one of the floating logs.

"I c'n walk 'em, too," he said, "as good as Robert Ireton."

"Well, don't you try it, mister," Caddie advised.

Now Robert had reached his log and mounted it. His feet were light and quick on the rolling log. He might have been dancing one of his Irish jigs on the threshing floor of the barn at home, to see him lift his feet. The water flashed and sparkled over the rolling log. Everybody was looking at him. He was better, more light and graceful, than the lumbermen from up the river.

But suddenly, in the midst of her pleasure and excitement at Robert's success, Caddie saw out of the tail of her eye that another log walker was performing near at hand. Ezra McCantry was stepping gingerly from log to log, and running the length of them and back with arms outstretched to keep his balance.

"Come back here, Ezra!" Caddie cried.

But Ezra only ran a little farther out and called back mockingly, "Look at me! Look at me! I c'n walk 'em, too!"

"Oh, dear!" Caddie said to Katie. "I just wish Emma had come down with us. She'd make him come back in pretty smart, I guess!"

Katie raised her gentle voice and called him, too, but Ezra was puffed up by the importance of the moment to even greater feats of daring. It seemed to him that everybody was looking at *him* now instead of Robert Ireton.

"Look-it me now! Look-it—"

Even as he uttered his howl of triumph, the log he was on began to roll. Slowly and gently it rolled, but it took Ezra by surprise and he rolled with it. He made a wonderful, big splash for such a very small boy.

"*Oh, dear!*" cried Caddie. "*Oh, dear!*"— and all sorts of disconnected things went like a panic through her mind. "*Be swift, my soul.*

*Be jubilant, my feet. . . .* But, oh, my dress! Whatever happens, it must not get wet."

And then she saw Ezra coming up to the surface and clawing the air an instant, trying to catch the log—and going down again without having succeeded. She knew that the millpond was deep and that Ezra couldn't swim—and neither could she. She heard people behind her beginning to shout, and Katie bursting into tears. Then, before she knew it, her clean white slippers were stepping out on the first logs and then the next ones, and she was frantically untying the long piece of bunting which had been over her shoulder.

She heard her own voice calling, *"Ezra! Ezra!"*

When he came up again she was still calling, and somehow she got his attention and flung one end of the bunting near enough to his clutching hands so that he could grasp it.

As he went down again, clutching the bunting, it snapped out tight, like a kite string in the wind, and Caddie, holding the other end, felt the log she was on beginning to roll. She tried to make her feet go fast, like Robert's feet, in order to keep her balance; but still her log kept rolling, rolling—and the clean white slippers with the satin rosettes could

not go fast enough. There was a second wonderful splash—and it was Caddie Woodlawn!

But she never let go of the bunting; and
Ezra was holding on to his end, too. There
was a log between them, and with the bunting
over it neither one of them could go down too
far. Caddie struggled desperately up until she
could cling to the log with one hand and pull
in the bunting with the other, and presently
Ezra was clinging to the other side of the log,
coughing and blowing water. With one on
each side of it the log had stopped rolling, and
they could hold to it and catch their breath
for a moment until help came.

Robert was the first to reach them, swimming from his log in mid-pond with long,
sure strokes.

"Oh, Robert!" Caddie cried, between gulps
and coughs. "You had to get off your log! We
made you lose the contest, Robert."

"Eh, divil take the contest," Robert roared,
"and my Caddie drowning! What do you
think, lass? What do you think!"

When they were safe on shore again, with
the water running from them in streams and
an anxious crowd surging around them, Caddie looked down and saw that she was still
clutching the Fourth of July bunting against
her breast. The red and blue dye was running

in gaudy little streams all down the front of her lovely new white dress. As she stood there speechless with this new calamity which topped all the others, she heard the first notes of the fife and drum calling the people to the speaking and the singing.

The crowd began to drift away, now that they saw Caddie and Ezra safe.

"Oh, come along now, Caddie," Katie said. "You'll dry out on the speakers' stand, with all the hot sun blazing in there. It's time we went to sing."

"But I can't! I can't—*like this,*" wailed Caddie.

Tom and Katie, Warren and Hetty and little Minnie were all around her, helping her wring out the yards of white—and *blue* and *red*—muslin.

"Sure you can, Caddie," they were saying. "They need your high voice on the choruses."

"You can sit in the back," said Katie, "and I'll spread my skirts out over yours."

"But Mother!" gasped Caddie. "She'll take one look at me and have a heart attack."

"You come along," they said.

Caddie and Katie had just time to squeeze in among the other girls at the back of the platform before the program began. Caddie was sure that Mother could not have seen the dreadful mess she was wearing.

When the fifes and drums were silent, the girls' chorus stood up and began to sing. Caddie remained seated so that she would not spoil the beautiful appearance of the other girls, but her voice soared clear and happy.

It seemed as if half of the men of Dunnville and Eau Galle made speeches that day, but Dr. Nightingale made the last one, and it was the best one, too. He spoke very simply, as if he were talking to friends—as, indeed, he was. He said that the truest way citizens could serve their country was by obeying its laws and by meeting daily life with courage and honesty. Good citizens, he said, were worth more to a nation than good soldiers or good policemen.

Caddie forgot her troubles in listening to his earnest voice. Finally he said something which surprised her.

He said, "There are many good citizens among us, but it has just been called to my attention that one of us today has proven particularly worthy of citizenship. This person, although one of the youngest members of our society, has proven equal to an emergency which called for quick thinking, courage, and a willingness to risk personal safety. You all know this young person; you have just heard her voice in the singing. When you know that Caddie Woodlawn saved a little boy's life this morning, I think you will want her to step forward and receive your cheers."

Until her name was mentioned, Caddie had been looking around trying to imagine whom Dr. Nightingale was speaking of. Now when she heard him saying "Will Caddie Woodlawn please come forward?" Caddie was so filled with astonishment and alarm that she could do nothing but sit there and whisper, "Oh, I can't!"

There was a great wave of cheering and applause, which frightened her even more. But the girls were pulling her to her feet.

"Don't be silly," they cried, pushing her forward.

To her surprise Caddie found herself going up to the front of the platform where Dr. Nightingale stood with outstretched hand and welcoming smile. Caddie had tried to hold the worst parts of her bedraggled skirt together so that it would not show, but when she held out her hand it all fell open so that everyone in Dunnville and Eau Galle could see that Caddie Woodlawn had spoiled another white dress.

Dr. Nightingale seemed to understand her distress just as he understood measles or mumps.

"Congratulations, Caddie," he said, "and

don't be ashamed of your dress, my dear. I'm proud to shake the hand of a girl who can forget her vanity to risk her life for others."

Caddie looked up at him in pleased surprise and then down to the blur of faces below her; and suddenly two faces stood out clearly. Mother and Father were sitting side by side, and both of their faces were full of pride and happiness. Even on Mother's handsome face there lingered not a trace of regret or reproach for the beautiful white dress which Caddie had ruined.

Well, it was a lovely day—a day to remember all one's life!

Caddie did not roll logs or chase the greased pig nor climb the greased pole, but even in her bedraggled dress she had a lovely time. And, better than doing it herself, she saw Tom scale the slippery pole and win the ham, and saw Robert Ireton outlast the men from the lumber camps and win the five-dollar gold piece for staying longest on his log. For everyone had agreed that he should not be disqualified from entering the final contest because he had jumped off his log in the morning to go to the assistance of Caddie and Ezra.

In the evening they all rode home on the hayload, tired but content, and as they rode they sang. An early moon was in the sky, and the odors of sweet clover and red clover and new-cut hay and pine mingled like perfume in the clear air.

> I've been roaming, I've been roaming,
> By the rose and lily fair,
> And I'm coming, and I'm coming,
> With their blossoms in my hair.
> Over hill and over plain
> To my bower back again,
> And I'm coming, and I'm coming,
> To my bower back again.

And, when the song had drifted away again to silence, Caddie found herself softly humming the other tune which seemed so perfectly to fit the day, and the new, sweet country which they loved so well.

> Oh, be swift, my soul, to answer Him!
> Be jubilant, my feet!